SEA OTTERS GAMBOLLING IN THE WILD, WILD SURF

John Bennett comes from the north-east of Scotland.
This is his first novel.

John Bennett

SEA OTTERS
GAMBOLLING IN THE
WILD, WILD SURF

VINTAGE BOOKS
London

Published by Vintage 2006
4 6 8 10 9 7 5 3

First published in Great Britain in 2006 by Vintage

Vintage
Random House, 20 Vauxhall Bridge Road,
London SW1V 2SA

Random House Australia (Pty) Limited
20 Alfred Street, Milsons Point, Sydney,
New South Wales 2061, Australia

Random House New Zealand Limited
18 Poland Road, Glenfield,
Auckland 10, New Zealand

Random House (Pty) Limited
Isle of Houghton, Corner of Boundary Road
& Carse O'Gowrie, Houghton 2198, South Africa

The Random House Group Limited Reg. No. 954009
www.randomhouse.co.uk/vintage

A CIP catalogue record for this book
is available from the British Library

ISBN 9780099490739 (from Jan 2007)
ISBN 0099490730

Papers used by Random House are natural, recyclable products
made from wood grown in sustainable forests. The manufacturing
processes conform to the environmental regulations of
the country of origin

Typeset by Palimpsest Book Production Limited,
Polmont, Stirlingshire

Printed and bound in Great Britain by
Cox & Wyman Ltd, Reading, Berkshire

To Charlotte

As I write this I'm hurtling through the infinite, velvety dark of the lower troposphere, 30,000 feet above the Indian subcontinent. Next to me Dennis is snoring like a madman.

I know India is below because for the last half hour I've been watching a little white icon of a plane creeping slowly across a map on the screen in front of me. Right now we're just coming up to Hyderabad.

Whatever.

While I've been watching the screen I've been trying to work out exactly how I got here. It's pretty complicated, but I suppose if you go back to the beginning it's because Vespasian, Mrs Pretzel's Cavalier King Charles Spaniel, had a prolapse two days ago.

*

When I woke up yesterday I was still feeling pretty monged from the night before. I poked my head out from under the duvet and looked at the alarm clock. It was 11.56, technically speaking still morning, though I'm sure my mother wouldn't have seen it that way, but as she and her best friend Sandra had left the day before for a fly/drive holiday on the Eastern Seaboard of the US it

3

was totally irrelevant. I turned over and went straight back to sleep.

Which was a big mistake because I dreamed of my 'A' Levels. Again.

It was the same setting, the dusty gym hall lined with wall bars, full of the pissy stench of teenage fear and the acrid honk of sweaty socks. On the desk in front of me sat the paper; I turned it over and read the first question:

If you differentiate all the occurrences of onomatopoeia in the first act of *Hamlet* correlated with the effects of transhumance on the Treaty of Versailles divided by the number of hectares in the islet of Langerhans, factored by the incidence of eskers in the Haber Process: what is the value of X?

I was like, 'What. The. Fuck?' I looked round; everyone else was writing. I didn't even know where to begin. The question didn't make any sense. I tried to remember what onomatopoeia was. Suddenly this insistent, tick-tock quiz-show music started playing in the background. Surely, I thought, it can't be over already. The girl next to me stopped writing and sat back in her chair with a smug look on her face. A feeling of panic welled up from my stomach into my chest. The music rose to a climactic finale and . . . I woke up in a tangle of sweaty sheets. It was almost two months since my last exam, but still they haunted my dreams.

I sat up and tried to forget the nightmare. Sun pissed into my room through the gaps in the blinds and collected in a soggy puddle at the end of my bed. I propped myself up on a couple of pillows and lay back with my hands behind my head, watching tiny motes of dust drift in the air, spiralling in the updrafts above the vast, jagged, Himalayan peaks of my duvet, like the souls of the dead or something.

As I lay watching the dust, I started to construct a plan to rid the world of any trace of eskers, so that those coming after me would not be forced to learn about the fucking things. I figured all I'd need was a ton of money and some bulldozers, but then, just as I'd convinced myself that I'd cracked the logistical issues, it occurred to me that I'd also need a strategy to stop them being taught about in a historical sense and I was starting to consider brainwashing tactics and mass hypnosis when I realised that the whole thing was a little obtuse to be truly sustaining or keep me from the inescapable fact that I was bored. Chairman of the fucking bored. If there was a religion based on boredom, I'd have been its pope. The High Pontiff of the Church of the Grand Ennui. People would have had to kiss my ring.

Actually, instead of mouldering in my scratcher that sunny summer's afternoon, I was supposed to be working for Mrs Pretzel, but the mad old crow had called the night before and cancelled work until further notice on account of her having to deal with Vespasian's intestinal issue.

I'd been working for Mrs Pretzel for a couple of months, though it's not like I wanted to or anything. After I finished my exams I'd totally intended to kick back and take it easy, figuring that I'd earned myself a little break. My mother had other plans. She gave me like one fucking day off after my final exam before she started nagging me to get a job.

'Felix, before you get comfortable, I want to make it absolutely clear that you are not hanging around this house watching television and playing video games for three months until you start university. You are going to do something constructive with your time.'

I managed to fend her off for about two weeks with a vague and entirely fabricated story about the possibility of some work in a supermarket, and I was just starting to think that maybe she'd forgotten about the whole thing, when she came home one day and announced that she was cutting off my allowance. Completely. No grace period, no nothing. I protested. She stood firm. However, she hadn't reckoned on the sheer scale of my slackness and, as she could barely refuse to feed me, the whole thing resulted in one mother-fucker of a Mexican stand-off. I spent the next week avoiding her, lounging around the house during the day and then heading round to my mate Jim's just before she got home, only returning in the early hours of the morning when I knew she'd be asleep. The plan was working pretty well until she ambushed me in my crib one morning.

'Felix, wake up.'

'Urrr . . .' I moaned dramatically, in an attempt to convey that by waking me and continuing to talk to me she might actually be endangering my life.

'Felix, stop that groaning and listen to me. I've got you a job.'

I turned over and sat up.

'Yes . . . good . . . I thought that might get your attention. I spoke to Dora last night at my Women of Achievement meeting and it turns out that she's looking for someone to tidy up her mother-in-law's garden. I volunteered your services. You start tomorrow.'

'But Mummmm . . .'

'And, Felix, if you lose this job in any way or for any reason, you are going to be in so much trouble that you'll wish you hadn't been born.' Which, if you think about it, is a funny sort of thing for a mother to say to her only son.

Whatever. I tried, I mean, you should have seen how hard I tried to get out of taking the job, but there was no escape, my mother is just not the kind of person who takes no for an answer. Resistance is futile.

That was several weeks ago, but now the thing was that as I lay in bed and watched the dust float around my room, I sort of wished I was at work. I don't want to go totally overboard here, but I was kind of missing the job. I suppose, if I could have been arsed, I would have been inclined to call my situation ironic.

Mrs Pretzel lives in one of the big, old houses round the corner. Mrs Pretzel is also crazy in the coconut, something it didn't take me very long to work out.

I rocked up at Mrs P's gaff on my first day and rang the bell, five minutes later nothing had happened and I was just about to sack it and head over to Jim's, when I heard some faint scrabbling followed by the complaining rasp of a lock. As I watched, the heavy door opened a little, and a small, wizened face appeared, hovering over the thick, brass security chain which spanned the dark gap between door and frame.

'Who are you and what do you want?' snapped the living fossil in the doorway.

Mrs Pretzel, for it was she, is a short woman. From what I could see she was wearing this high-collared, black dress made out of some heavy, old-skool, velvety material. She had about two tons of make-up plastered on her massively wrinkled face, which did nothing to disguise the fact that she looked like she'd been around since the last ice age.

'I'm Felix and I've come to help in your garden . . . my mother arranged it with Dora,' I said brightly, 'you, know, your daughter-in-law . . .'

'Yes, I know very well who my daughter-in-law is, thank you,' she snapped sharply.

'Oh, uh, yeah,' I mumbled apologetically.

'But how do I know you are who you say you are?' she asked, staring at me suspiciously with her beady little eyes.

'Well . . . who else would know that I was supposed to come round . . .'

'Anyone could have picked up that information,' she said, 'and a woman of my age has to be careful. There are all sorts of rapists, perverts and molesters out there.'

I was like, 'In your dreams.'

'Look, if you want, you can phone Dora, or my mother . . . they'll vouch for me.'

'Have you got some identification?' she asked, still eyeing me charily.

I dug in my pocket, pulled out my wallet, extracted my school library card and handed it to her. She grabbed it with her withered little claw, examined it carefully in the light of the doorway before pronouncing it a fake. I was about to tell her to stick her job where the sun don't shine when she closed the door in my face. For the second

8

time I considered sacking it and heading off to Jim's, but I knew if I did my mother would bust me so hard that the rest of the summer would be a total write-off. I stood there, not knowing what to do, getting more and more pissed off with her for not letting me do a job I didn't want to do in the first place, and then getting even more pissed off that I was letting this whole scenario piss me off . . . when suddenly the door swung open.

The narrow porch opened out into a large, gloomy hallway; muscular, Victorian furniture lurked threateningly in the shadows, a couple of spiteful-looking aspidistras stood guard at the bottom of the stairs. The air was damp and musty, and the whole place had a kind of catty smell. Mrs Pretzel handed back the library card.

'Before you start on the garden, Felix, I must introduce you to my husband, Aubrey. He's in the drawing room.'

I was a little perplexed. I didn't remember my mother saying Mrs Pretzel had a husband; in fact, as I remembered it, my mother had said she was on her own, which was why she needed help in the first place.

The drawing room was pretty dark. Heavy curtains, which appeared to be made out of the same material as Mrs Pretzel's dress, blocked out most of the light. Phantasmal furniture, draped in dust sheets, skulked in the sepulchral gloom. I saw no sign of Aubrey.

'Aubrey,' said Mrs P, 'this is Felix. He's the boy I was telling you about, the one who's come to do the garden.'

Boy? I mean, I was going to say something, but I thought better of it.

'Felix, this is Aubrey, he says hello.'

I looked over at Mrs Pretzel, who was staring at the fireplace directly in front of us. I followed her gaze. On

9

the mantelpiece stood an ornate stone urn. I stepped forward to get a better look. The urn was surrounded by a host of pictures of this totally furtive looking individual, who seemed to be trying to hide behind a mouldy old handlebar moustache festering on his top lip. Mrs Pretzel turned to me with a sort of expectant look in her eye and nodded at the urn.

'Er . . . hello, Aubrey . . . I'm Felix,' I said hesitantly. It was totally weird, but what was I going to do? Looking back, I should have bailed then.

Now when my mother 'sold' me the job she said something like, 'Felix, there's an old lady who needs a little help to tidy up her garden.'

As I stepped through the decaying, wooden patio doors into the garden, I realised that when my mother said 'tidy up' she was about a million miles off the mark. It's like saying that Hiroshima needed a bit of a 'tidy up' after the Americans dropped the Big One.

The French windows opened onto a ruined patio on which stood a peeling, wrought-iron garden table covered in suppurating, red rust sores and a couple of similarly afflicted chairs, surrounded by a dense, suffocating wall of plant life. I'm not exaggerating when I say that the garden was one of the world's last great undiscovered wildernesses. I could see that I wasn't going to be gardening; I was going to be making a journey into the heart of fucking darkness.

On the table sat a bottle of supermarket own-brand sherry, a murky tumbler, a pack of Peter Stuvyesant and a copy of the *Daily Mail*. Mrs Pretzel sat down on one of the chairs, poured herself a glass of sherry and sparked up.

'Sit, sit,' she said, before knocking back her sherry and pouring herself a second.

As I was making myself comfortable, a rustling from the edge of the patio caught my attention; I turned to see a dog's backside protruding from a slug-ravaged border. Mrs Pretzel took a little sip on her cigarette, almost immediately sending a thin jet of smoke skywards.

'Before we discuss the details of your employ, you must allow me to introduce you to Vespasian,' she said, motioning towards the dog's butt with a regal flick of her hand. 'Vespasian, come and meet Felix.' The dog totally ignored her and continued moping around in the undergrowth.

'Why's he called Vespasian?' I asked, still labouring under the mistaken impression that Mrs Pretzel maintained at least a slim grasp on reality.

'Vespasian was the emperor who restored stability to Rome after the death of Nero,' she said enigmatically. I was like, 'Right.' Did that mean Aubrey was her Nero?

In the following weeks Mrs Pretzel was pretty tight-lipped on the subject of Aubrey. I never discovered how he died or anything. Though, if you asked me to guess, I'd say it was by his own hand. I know I fucking would have if I was married to the old gibbon.

Whatever. Despite the fact that the dog had just completely ignored her, Mrs Pretzel launched into this total paean to the creature. She went on and on, crediting the mutt with all sorts of abilities. From the way she told it Vespasian could have led the country if it hadn't been for some unlucky breaks.

'Yes, Felix, Vespasian is a natural leader, when you see him in the company of other dogs you will understand

11

immediately.' The dim-witted pooch removed its head from the foliage and looked up at me with its soppy eyes.

'A bit of a Tony Blair?' I asked innocently, in an attempt at some adult-friendly bullshit.

'Oh, no, no, no, no, no,' moaned Mrs Pretzel, before lungeing down and scooping up the hapless hound, which had wandered over in our direction. 'Don't listen to the nasty boy,' she cooed, clamping her hands over its floppy saddlebag ears.

'Tony Blair is the most evil man in Britain; he intends to tax the old and weak and take all our money. Vespasian is a defender of the weak and old, aren't you Vespasian?'

What did I tell you? Loop the fucking loop. Anyway, then she went into this whole wounded bird act, gazing mournfully into the middle distance whilst hosing back a couple of big glasses of sherry, like she was drinking brandy from the barrel on the neck of a St Bernard after a close shave with an avalanche or an esker or something.

'Yes, Felix,' she said eventually, the sherry having worked its cut-price magic, 'I haven't touched the garden since the day Aubrey died . . . it will be fifteen years next March.'

'Have you ever thought about hiring a professional gardener?' I asked in my most helpful voice, hoping that this might prove to be a revelation, like maybe she'd say, 'Why Felix, I hadn't thought of that, how clever of you, I'll phone one now . . .' but then, as she picked up the phone, it would dawn on her that she would have to lay me off, so then she'd make to put the phone down, but I'd stop her and say, 'No, it's for the best, it's a job for

12

a professional,' and then she'd insist on paying me for the next two weeks and . . .

'Gardener?' she screeched incredulously, as if I'd asked her if she'd ever thought about indulging in some monstrous sexual practice. 'Gardener,' she said again, choking slightly this time, like a cat coughing up a hairball, 'Felix, let me tell you about gardeners.'

Which she did. At great length. According to her all gardeners are cheats and thieves who rob, overcharge and trick old women just for kicks; in her book there's no difference between gardeners and her unholy trinity of rapists, perverts and molesters.

'But why are you hiring me?' I asked when she'd finished her tirade, sensing that if I could perhaps align myself with the gardening fraternity in her mind she might turn against me and dispense with my services.

'A good question Felix,' she replied, eyeing me with suspicion, 'I must confess to having manifold doubts about your honesty and integrity and it is also clear to me from what your mother says that you are an unfocussed individual. However, both Aubrey and I feel that a dose of honest manual labour may help build some character, and, as my dear departed husband Aubrey always used to say, character determines fate.'

I was outraged. She made it sound like *she* was doing *me* some sort of favour. Plus what was all that guff about character and fate?

'Yes, Felix, I could sense that Aubrey shared many of my reservations about your general character and ability, but despite that, I think we will take you on . . . on a trial basis.'

Which, even disregarding her seemingly miraculous

13

ability to communicate with her dead husband, was total bullshit. I knew that the only reason I was working for the old iguanodon was because my mother had hired my arse out at virtual slave-labour rates. I mean, a tenner a day, what the fuck's that about?

Even then, I wouldn't have minded so much, if:

(a) I hadn't known that the old viper was as rich as Croesus; or
(b she hadn't cheated me out of my rightful pay.

For some unexplained reason Mrs Pretzel paid me at the end of every day. Actually, I was pretty happy when she informed me about this arrangement because it meant that I'd get my hands on some money straight off instead of having to wait for ages like with most other jobs. However, when she called me into the house to pay me after I finished the first day, I got a nasty surprise in the form of a big pile of one and two pences sitting on the kitchen table.

After taking an age to count it out, the whole lot came to the grand total of £7.08.

'I'm sorry, Mrs Pretzel, but I think you've made a mistake, there's only seven pounds here and my mother agreed it would be ten.' Her eyes screwed up like two squashed flies.

'Now, sonny, just because I'm an old woman, don't be thinking you can get one over on me, I might be a little bent and bowed, but it's all still in full working order up here,' she said tapping her forehead. OK, so she may be insane-in-da-membrane, but she's not fucking stupid.

*   *   *

'I'm not doing that again,' I said emphatically. My mother turned round from the dishwasher.

'What do you mean?' she asked, her eyes narrowing like she was Clint fucking Eastwood.

'Um, well, you know we agreed that she would pay me ten pounds a day?'

'Yesss,' my mother said, her hand moving slowly to her holster.

'Well, she totally diddled me, she only paid me like seven . . .' A vulture circled overhead in the cloudless desert sky.

'She's an old woman, she's probably just a little confused. I hope you didn't cause a fuss . . .'

'No, Mum, but she promised, that was the deal . . .' Like a rattlesnake striking, her hands shot to her gun, in a blur of smoke the bullets crashed into my stomach.

'Well, I'm sure it was just a mistake, I think you should let it go this once.' A gut shot, guaranteed death out here. Blood trickled through my fingers; I looked up at the sky, where a minute ago there was one vulture, now suddenly there were three, wheeling in long, languorous loops.

'Ahh, Mum . . . well, I'm not doing it, I'm not working for nothing.'

'Felix, she's an old lady, helping her should be a reward in itself,' and that was that. The coup de grâce.

After that it only got worse. The old bat gradually knocked off more and more money here and there. My last pay for a full day's work was £4.20 mixed in with some old half pences which she insisted were still legal tender. The day before she even had the neck to give me some pre-decimal coins, which she insisted were valuable collector's items and worth a good deal more than their face value. When I complained she threatened to phone my mother and then started prattling on about how I'd only play ducks and drakes with the extra money. Whatever the fuck that means.

I mean, £4.20 for a full day's labouring in her garden, it's a total joke, and what makes it even more frustrating is the fact that whilst I've been working for a pittance for this loony old woman, my mates have been sitting around smoking draw and generally enjoying their last summer of freedom.

I sat up, leaned out of bed, retrieved my mobile from the floor and switched it on. There was one text. It was from Rob asking me to call him.

Rob, aka The Plague, is my oldest friend. We went to playschool together. His mum's big buddies with mine. Nowadays, however, we don't really have that much in common other than lots of embarrassing photos of us playing together in various paddling pools and sandpits when we were three or whatever. In fact, the only reason I still have anything to do with him is because he buys our drugs for us. I called him.

'Rob, it's Felix.'

'Arse . . .'

Arse is my nickname; I'm sure you can work out why. Kids are such bastards. Though I suppose it's really my parents' fault for giving me a stupid name. In France, and I swear this is one hundred per cent true, there's an official list and parents have got to pick their kid's name from it. They should do that here. The other option would be to give kids the legal right to change their own names when they're like nine or something, but I'm not so sure

16

that's a great idea. If I'd been allowed to change my name when I was that age there's a fair chance that I'd now be called The Undertaker or Chewbacca or something.

'Whhhappen . . . blood,' Rob drawled.

'Rob, why'd you text me?' I asked, ignoring his pathetic attempts to sound like some bad-ass rudebwoy.

'Party, innit.'

'What?'

'There's a party tonight at Jessica's house, man. Her parents are in the BVIs, I'm doing a set . . . it's going to kick off big time.'

'Yeah . . . and?'

'So you need anything, bruv?'

When Rob says anything, he means party drugs, but he doesn't like to discuss such matters directly on the phone in case it's tapped. Which is a little unlikely as Rob isn't exactly Scarface, though he does own the DVD. I mean, he's such a fucking dick; seriously, he acts like he's the motherfucking O.G., just because he spins around on a Gilera and deals to his mates. All of which is made even more laughable given that:

(a) he goes to the same public school as me; and
(b) his father is a partner in one of the biggest accountancy practices in the City.

'Um yes, get me whatever Jim is having,' I replied, playing along with his little charade. He was, after all, going to get the drugs so I didn't want to piss him off unduly and miss out on the fun. For the same reason, he doesn't know that Jim and I call him The Plague.

* * *

After I finished talking to Rob on the phone, I lay back and scanned my bedroom for something to do. It was littered with the usual adolescent props, a guitar with three strings missing and an artfully scuffed skateboard poked out of a fetid stew of magazines, broken CD cases, and dirty clothes. Unfortunately, I can't play the guitar, unless you count 'Twinkle, Twinkle Little Star' or the chorus of 'Smells Like Teen Spirit', and my skating ability just about extends to dodging dogshit, but if you're a teenage boy, you're pretty much compelled to buy the right gear, and who am I to rock the boat?

Whatever.

As I scanned the debris on my bedroom floor, I spotted an empty Coke can, with a half-smoked blunt from the night before perched on the edge minding its own business. I briefly contemplated sparking up, but then I decided to sack it. I had a hectic day in front of me and the last thing I needed was weed . . .

After I'd finished the joint, I lay in my pit for a while feeling all relaxed and fuzzy, and I could have probably lain there all day, but eventually the smell of my own farts seeping up from under the duvet became so disgusting I was forced to make a dash for the escape module and abandon the mothership.

In the shower I was overtaken by horniness so I cracked one off, blasting my man-fat all over the Burnished Peach tiling. I know it's Burnished Peach because my mother spent forever talking about it, looking through endless colour swatches, gauging family opinion and then trying to 'source' the exact colour for the 'project'.

She's totally addicted to those property shows on the

18

telly, and in the last couple of years there's not a room in the house which hasn't been subjected to some sort of 'makeover'. I despise those programmes, you know the ones, where they get some preposterous ponce and a stick insect woman, who evidently spends most of her time with her fingers down her throat, to come in and totally disparage someone's kitchen. Then, after making sure we all know how uncool it is, they charge off and replace it with another one which they *bought from a shop*. Then they act like they just split the fucking atom. What's that about? And what's wrong with Artex anyway? I once had a dream about a big monkey that lived in space and then one day he came to earth and Artexed the whole sky. It was a pretty cool effect. Plus, at some point in the future, Artex will be back like a motherfucker and all those dullards who ripped it off their walls and ceilings will be queuing up like lemmings at the counters of DIY stores throughout the land to buy the stuff again, because some other stick insect woman has told them it's the latest thing, and there are only so many ideas on the face of this dying planet.

Actually, in the end, I'm glad she chose Burnished Peach, because it shows up the man-fat better than the white tiling we had before and I'm a little paranoid about someone finding one of my abstract expressionist works splattered on the wall. Let's face it, the shower's the best place for a wank, but there is the drawback that on contact with water, man-fat adopts the consistency of superglue. Every morning I have to spend a couple of minutes hosing down the Burnished Peach with the shower turned up full to get rid of the evidence.

*   *   *

In the kitchen, refreshed and ready for what was left of the day ahead, I assembled a late lunch of crisps and a choc ice and settled down at the breakfast bar. As I opened the bag of crisps, my mobile rang.

'Felix . . . just because I'm old doesn't mean I've forgotten how to please a man.'

It was Jim, doing a horrible old woman impersonation of what he likes to make out goes on between myself and the good Mrs Pretzel.

Jim is my best mate, though we haven't actually been friends that long. When he moved to my school a couple of years ago, he was dragged round my house by his mother, who met my mother at some Women of Achievement event. They'd decided that, as Jim and I were in the same year, we should be forced to be friends. I can't say I was looking forward to it much, and when Jim pitched up I was like 'there's no way we're going to get on'.

Jim's a total indie boy, you know the kind . . . the skinny, pallid ones you see mooching round Camden wearing sixties retro gear and carrying bags full of obscure second-hand vinyl.

Whatever.

In those days I spent most of my time hanging out with my Computer Club homies. Don't get me wrong, they're good guys and I'm still pretty friendly with them, but they're not cool, unless of course you think being down with the Linux kernel or being in a *Quake* clan is cool. Take Kevin, for example: OK, his IQ is the size of the Death Star, but then so is he. I mean, he's only seventeen but I think he's almost twenty stone. Which is pretty bad, because I know that deep down he really wants to be an elf. His main *Everquest* characters are always elves and he collects all this weirdo *LOTR* memorabilia off the internet. Now, I'm not one hundred per cent sure, but I don't think there were any morbidly obese elves in Middle Earth, but then I guess they didn't live on Pringles, unlike Kevin.

Whatever.

For the first hour or so Jim talked about all these bands and films that I'd never even heard of and when I put on an Eminem album he totally turned his nose up at it. In fact, it wasn't until I put on 'Get Off of My Cloud' by the Stones, as a subtle hint, that Jim perked up. It turned out that he was massively into the Stones as well.

I'm into the Stones because my dad's a huge fan. He'd seen them like five times, back in the seventies, and when I told Jim that he got pretty excited, he even said he was jealous, because his dad is into classical music and would never have done anything as cool as go and see the Stones. Which was kind of strange, I'd never really thought of my dad as being cool before.

'Just because there's snow on the roof, doesn't mean there isn't a fire roaring in the grate.'

'Jim,' I said harshly.

'OK. Chill Felix, it's a joke.'

'Sorry, it's just that I'm still a little tired after last night.' We'd stayed up until four playing *GTA III* on my PS2 and smoking copious amounts of weed.

'Yeah, me too,' said Jim, yawning loudly down the phone in sympathy.

'What's your plan?' I asked.

'Hmm, dunno, I promised my mother that I'd wash

her car, but I've subcontracted that job to the squeeb next door. So theoretically, I'm free.'

'Look, what say we meet in town, I've got the money for the trainers now.'

I'd been saving for a new pair of trainers for ages, because my old ones were falling to pieces. I know that can sometimes be a good look, but trust me these ones had left the fashionably distressed phase behind some time ago.

It had taken me ages to save the cash for the trainers because my only source of income was what I earned from my job at Mrs Pretzel's, and, as you already know, that was a totally derisory amount.

Jim, on the other hand, is minted. He lives in a big villa in this gated development down by the river; his dad is European vice president in charge of raping the Third World or something at one of the mega oil companies. His parents give him this huge monthly allowance, and pay his mobile bills. Plus he gets to drive his mother's Beemer most of the time.

I don't want to complain too much, I'm not exactly on the street, but you know, it's a bit of a pain being skint. I suppose it's all relative, but still, it doesn't make it any easier when Jim can afford to buy stuff and do things that I can't.

Jim paused for a second, 'Sure, look, I'll see you outside Maccy Ds around threeish.'

After Jim hung up, I finished my choc ice, which was quite difficult because it had melted and I had to slurp it off the wrapper. Then I got my shit together and headed out.

*   *   *

22

I'm not seventeen yet, which means that while all my friends are zooming about in their parents' cars, I'm still condemned to blagging lifts or hanging around in windy bus shelters and train stations, at the mercy of this country's crumbling public transport system. I know, you're thinking what's he doing sitting his 'A' Levels if he's not even seventeen? The reason is that I was put forward a year in primary school because I was judged to be 'intellectually gifted'. Which means that I sat my 'A' Levels over a year early.

Whatever.

As luck would have it, as I walked down the front garden into the close outside the house Julie from over the road pulled out of her drive. She spotted me and wound down her window.

'You going into town Felix?'

'Yeah.'

'Want a lift?'

Which was a total result, because Julie is seriously hot. I fancy her big time. She frequently features in my sexual fantasies, though I'll spare you the details. Unfortunately, she's married to Tim, who's ten years older than her, fat, bald and most probably a sexual deviant. He's the manager of a contract cleaning company. She was his secretary. I invite you to draw your own conclusions about the basis and nature of their relationship.

'How are you Felix?'

'Oh, good . . . you know.'

She was wearing a pair of sheer black tights, a figure-hugging black skirt and a floaty, translucent white blouse, through which I could just about discern the fine, lacy tracery of her bra.

'So, what are you doing? Off to see the girlfriend, eh?' she said, winking. OK, so I know she married Tim just under two years ago and all that, but she flirts with me massively. I swear, I'm not making this up. I reckon she knows I fancy her (I think it's the drooling and the hunchback gait that gives me away), she's flattered by the attention, so she flirts back, thinking maybe it's a bit of harmless fun.

'No . . . no,' I replied, surreptitiously pulling the bottom of my hoody down to cover my incipient boner as I got into the car.

'So, are you seeing someone steady?' she continued, as I closed the door and put on my seat belt.

'No . . . no one,' I replied, trying to convey by the cool tone of my voice that I remained single because, despite being inundated with offers, I *chose* to remain footloose and fancy free, not because women wouldn't go anywhere near me. As we talked I noticed that she was holding the handbrake, her thumb wandering aimlessly over the sleek, black button at the end.

'A girl in every port, eh?' she replied, releasing the brake before taking a firm yet delicate grip of the thick, leather-covered gear stick and slipping the car into first. Then she stamped on the accelerator and gunned it down the close. OK, so she may be cute, but her driving is pretty fucked up.

'Well not quite,' I said, 'we're over thirty miles from the sea.' A lame joke, but she giggled as she leaned over and switched on the CD player, filling the car with Dido's bland warbling. On the face of it a serious crime against good taste, but considering the defendant's spotless character and A1 knockers, one I was prepared to overlook.

'How come you're back from work?' I asked.

'I had to nip back home and sort out a guy who's doing some work on the boiler . . . pain in the arse really.' A five-second porn movie played in my head. I had a moustache. The boiler remained unfixed.

'You're off to university at the end of the summer aren't you?' she asked, swinging the car around the mini-round-about at the bottom of the close at an alarming speed, like it was a spaceship and she was using the gravitational field of the earth to slingshot us into outer space.

'Well, yes hopefully . . . I'm waiting for my "A" Level results,' I said, gripping the sides of the seat as she floored the accelerator.

'Do you think you did well?'

'Um, I suppose so . . . my mocks were OK.'

'Better than OK, going by what your mum had to say,' said Julie, smiling at me broadly.

'I guess . . .' I replied, ever so humble like.

'Well four As is about as good as it gets. What subjects did you do?'

'Maths, Physics, History and English.'

'And do you know where you're going yet?'

'I have a conditional to study commercial law at Cambridge.'

'Impressive,' she said, swerving and only narrowly avoiding this old fizzer who had the temerity to try and cross the road.

'Well it's not guaranteed, I still have to get the results,' I replied.

'You didn't fancy a gap year then?' asked Julie.

I was like 'No way.' I mean, for a start Prince William totally spoiled all the fun in that concept. After my mother saw him on telly she actually wanted me to go on one, she even had brochures and shit. Didn't she know that, as a teenager, I was duty bound to do my utmost to piss her off by doing the exact opposite of what she wanted, irrespective of whether that might actually be beneficial to me? And anyway, if I was shovelling shit on a farm in Australia, I'd probably be at the mercy of all sorts of inbred convicts with an eye for some fresh young arse. Plus, when it comes down to it, shovelling shit is shovelling shit, right? Whether it takes place in Chile or Wolver-fucking-hampton.

I suppose I could have gone for the other option of living on a beach in Thailand or some place for a year. I could have got some ratty dreads and a bongo drum and tried to fool myself that taking a shitload of drugs meant that I was on some sort of spiritual quest, and that the minging tattoos and septic piercings were tribal markings and a real expression of my alternative lifestyle. But to be honest that seems pretty much as lame as the first option. Plus, I don't see why having watched the sun rise over some ruined temple or hurling yourself off a bridge attached to a piece of elastic makes you some sort of superior individual.

Whatever.

I was about to answer when Julie tried to pull into the next lane without looking. A white van veered wickedly as it whizzed past, the horn wailing. I grabbed the dashboard. She didn't even bat an eyelid, like it never happened.

'So I hear you're having a little party on results day,' she continued, seemingly oblivious to the man in the passenger seat of the van who was now leaning out his window wanking off an invisible cock.

26

'Yeah it's not this Saturday, but the one after,' I said, feeling a little embarrassed.

'I thought your mum was away for a couple of weeks?'

'The party's on the day she gets back,' I explained.

It's true that my mother's arranged a 'little celebration party' for me when I get my results, like it's some foregone conclusion. She's invited all the people in the close. My little sister'll be back from her holiday at my dad's. Plus, she's invited all her friends from the charity and I think even a couple of aunts are coming over. What if I fail? Has she thought of that?

Julie turned and smiled, totally ignoring the road.

'Well, Tim and I will be there, we'll put the champagne on ice.'

'Jooollleee . . .' I shouted. She slammed on the brakes, stopping inches in front of this pedestrian crossing.

'You seem very tense Felix,' she said calmly.

Two main thoughts wove through my mind, like Sonic and Tails:

(a) God, she's hot;
(b) God, please let me live.

As we sat waiting for the lights to change, she hit the windscreen scooshers, they blasted their . . . oh man, I'm telling you, I was deeply, deeply conflicted. Half of me wanted to get out right there and then and the other half of me wanted the journey to go on for ever and ever and ever. But it didn't and before I knew it we were parked on the High Street and I was backing out of the car onto the pavement thanking her, whilst simultaneously

27

attempting to stare down her blouse and divert attention away from my, by now, raging boner.

I watched Julie spin off down the High Street and then took up position outside Maccy Ds, trying my best to look totally disaffected and disguise the fact that I still had the horn. My mobile went off.

'It is I, Jim.'

'Hey, vato.'

'Sorry Felix, I'm going to be late; my subcontracting scheme has backfired a little.'

'How?'

'The little germ's done a second-rate job and gone AWOL so I'm going to have to finish it myself. I'll be half an hour.'

'You just can't get the staff, these days,' I said, sympathetically.

'Tell me about it.'

Given that there was no way I could look disaffected for a whole half hour and that my boner had subsided just enough for me to walk upright, I decided to go for a wander. After getting some money out of the bank to pay for the trainers, I cruised up the High Street, past the prime sites occupied by Boots and Gap, into the retail hinterland of charity shops and dusty, family-owned businesses and I was about to head back into the centre of town when I noticed that one of my laces had come undone. I stopped and tied it. As I stood up I noticed a tatty canvas banner with the legend CLEARANCE SALE in tired red lettering hanging limply over the façade of the shop in front of me, covering the fixed sign of the previous tenant. In the window was a torn piece of cardboard box with ENDS TODAY – EVERYTHING MUST GO written on it in black marker pen.

It was one of those shops that you get in every high street where someone's hired empty premises for a week or a month or whatever and then filled it full of the cheapest, nastiest shit in the world. You know the kind; like a 99p shop but infinitely worse. It didn't seem to have a name or anything, but it should have been called The House of Ming.

To this day I don't know why I decided to go inside, maybe it was their sophisticated marketing tactics, maybe I'd just been caning the weed too hard. Who knows?

The interior of the House of Ming was total chaos. It was crammed full of overflowing cardboard boxes and cheap storage units covered in all sorts of junk. On the nearest shelf I could see a row of anti-dandruff shampoo next to some cut-glass swans, then there were some crystal therapy gift packs beside some toothpaste with Arabic script all over the box. Immediately in front of me stood a dump bin advertising the Rugrats movie; however, the bin itself was full of socks, not Rugrats socks, just black nylon socks selling at £1.99 for ten pairs. Slumped on the floor next to the dump bin sat a battered cardboard box full of books. I knelt down and had a quick rummage, hoping I might find something interesting, but it was full of celebrity autobiographies, diet books and self-help manuals; the usual cultural sewage. Anyway, I was just about to sack it and go and meet Jim when a massive tidal wave of nostalgia almost knocked me off my feet. Next to the books, propped against a grubby pillar, stood a pile of Sea Monkey kits. Sea Monkeys. I hadn't seen them for total yonks.

My sister got some when we were kids. I remember, as we put the plastic tank together, my sister, who is like three years younger than me, asked my mother if they were really monkeys.

'Yes,' my mother replied, smiling.

'No, they're not,' I said, ever the precocious little shit, 'they're brine shrimps, it says so on the box in the little writing.'

My mother looked at me. 'Well yes, but . . .'

'Why does it say they're monkeys, Mummy?' asked my sister.

My mother looked stumped, what could she say? Evil marketing droids? I think not.

'It's because they are sort of like monkeys, don't you think?' she said, shooting me a significant look. I don't remember if I said anything else, but probably not, my mother can be a scary motherfucker when she wants to be. However, I do remember that eventually the Sea Monkey water went bad, all brown and minging and it started to smell, like a cat had shit in it or something, so my mother poured the whole thing down the bog.

For about a nanosecond, I toyed with the idea of buying the Sea Monkeys as a sort of ironic purchase, but then I thought it might be more nostalgic than ironic and in the end it all seemed like too much responsibility to keep them so I put them back on the shelf.

Then I found it.

I stood and stared in amazement, barely able to believe my eyes. It was the most obscene thing I had ever seen.

What sat on the shelf before me was a plastic statuette, about eight inches high by ten inches long, depicting a fat, semi-naked, bald man rear-ending an oversized, pink, glittery otter. I stood there and gaped. I couldn't believe it. It was a statue of a man having sex with an otter. It was totally fucked up.

Relatively speaking the otter was enormous, its head height the same as the man's. I mean, I know nothing about otters, but the scale seemed seriously wrong.

The pink colour on the otter's body was graded, moving from hot fuchsia on its back to a light, little-girl pink on its underbelly. The paint had a soft, airbrushed finish and it was flecked with tiny specks of silver glitter, which made the otter's coat glisten as if it had just stepped out of the water. The texture of the fur had been rendered with such exquisite attention to detail that individual hairs were clearly discernible.

The man was wearing a manky string vest, pulled taut over his corpulent torso; again the detail was amazing. Rolls of fat hung around his stomach like apple strudel. A pair of grey trousers lay crumpled around his ankles, shit-streaked underpants just visible inside, his flaccid backside carefully rendered in an uncomfortably realistic flesh tone. He was all but bald, though he had attempted to disguise this with a combover, and a few wispy strands of hair covered his shiny pate, forlorn remnants of his male vanity. And his cock; you could just see the base of his cock where it entered the animal.

But, I tell you what though, the thing that freaked me out the most about the statuette was the look on the faces of the man and the otter. The man's face was caught at that moment just after ejaculation when the world comes back to you, that moment when the joy of release mixes with disgust at having just whacked off all over the computer keyboard or the Burnished Peach or whatever.

The otter, on the other hand, was grinning madly. Thick, full human lips revealing a set of perfect human teeth.

I looked along the shelf, to see if there were others, but it was the only one; the rest of the shelf was full of boxes of Bacon Rax™: With All New Crispotronic Technology. A lurid picture on the front of the box showed the circular plastic rack in front of a microwave, pink flaps of bacon hanging over it like severed ears. I picked up the figurine and made my way to the counter at the back of the shop.

The counter was a makeshift affair, constructed out of a sheet of plywood and two piles of breeze blocks. It was manned by a woman who looked like a troll. She wore a baggy, food-flecked fleece. Her face was puffy and white, her bleached blonde hair limp and frazzled. I rummaged in my smile drawer, pulled out my best one and flashed it at her.

'Hello, I wonder if you can help me,' I asked politely.

She looked at me impassively, idly scratching a livid scab on her forearm. Flakes of skin floated slowly downwards. I laid the statuette on the counter, careful to avoid the drift of dead skin.

'It's just I'm wondering where this came from?' I asked.

'What do you mean, mister, it came from 'ere. I just saw you pick it up,' she replied, eyeing the statuette with disgust.

32

'No, no, sorry, I'm not being clear. Where did it come from before? Where did you get it from?'

'Why?' she asked, looking at me suspiciously, 'Why do you want to know?'

'Don't worry, I'm just looking for the manufacturer, it's—'

'You're not Trading Standards are you?' she snapped defensively, 'Because if you are you'll have to speak with my husband.'

'No, no,' I protested.

'Tony,' she shouted through to the back of the shop, 'there's a bloke 'ere from Trading Standards.'

Now, I don't know how she got the fucked-up idea that I was from Trading Standards. Did she not see my hoody, jeans and high-tops? Did she not clock the circa 1972 Keith Richards hairdo? She was probably on tranquillisers or some other government-sponsored drug.

Before I had a chance to correct her, a middle-aged man stuck his head round the corner of the door. He had a thin, delicate face, and straggly, unkempt greying hair. Age-wise I would have said he was loitering around the fifty mark.

'What is it love?'

'He wants to know where this thing comes from,' she said, grimacing and pointing at the statuette, 'he's from the Trading Standards, he wants to close down the shop.'

Again, I tried to put her right, but she was off on one.

'I knew from the first time I clapped eyes on that thing that it would bring nothing but bad luck, but of course you knew better, all you can see is the short term, you never see the big picture, it's what my mother said before I even married you.'

Tony stepped into the shop. To my surprise he was quite fat; the contrast between the big goitre round his waist and his thin, delicate face was arresting. He wore a defeated brown cardigan, a faded LA Lakers T-shirt, black Adidas tracky bottoms and a pair of paint-spattered Timberlands. He looked like he came from a mountainous area of the remotest part of a hitherto undiscovered region of the land that fashion forgot.

'You don't look like you're from Trading Standards,' he said, ignoring the screeching hag beside him.

'I'm not from Trading Standards.'

'So why did you tell the wife you were?' asked Tony indignantly.

'I didn't, I merely asked about this . . . object, and your wife assumed the rest,' I replied trying to keep my cool.

'So what are you? Why do you want to know about this thing?'

'I just want to know where it came from . . . so I can order some more . . . I'm in the business.'

'A likely story, now hop it son, before I call the police. Coming in here, cheeking-up the wife, telling her you're from Trading Standards . . . I don't know, kids these days.'

'But I want to buy it as well,' I said trying to contain my exasperation.

Tony eyed me with suspicion. 'You want to buy it?'

'Yeah, I want to buy it,' I said, pulling my wallet out of my pocket, opening it and showing him the money I had for the trainers.

'Well why didn't you say so before sir,' he said unctuously, before turning and frowning at his wife. She said

34

nothing but puffed up her chest like one of those hens Foghorn Leghorn is always trying to poke.

He sighed and then smuggled me a little look which, if I read it right, said something like, 'Sorry 'bout the missus, but we're both men, I'm sure we can sort this out'. Then he fished in the pocket of his cardigan and pulled out a pair of half-moon spectacles. After he'd untangled them, he put them on and looked at the statuette.

'Oh, this,' he said thoughtfully, 'yes, this is a thoroughly disgusting object. I found it amongst a crate of the microwave bacon racks, which incidentally are one of our biggest sellers.'

'Yes,' I agreed, ignoring his aside about the bacon racks, 'I know the thing is an abomination, but the workmanship is very good. I've been looking for someone who can do this kind of work.'

Tony peered at the statuette again. 'Yes, well, I can see it has been well made. What business did you say you were in?'

'Oh . . . ornaments, objets d'art, that sort of thing.'

'I see, I see, we also have some rather attractive crystal swans, if you're interested, well, maybe not crystal, but definitely very high quality cut glass.'

'No, sorry, I'm only interested in the otter.'

'And you definitely want to buy it?' he asked. I nodded. Tony looked at his wife and smiled, his smile said, 'Big picture, big picture, big picture', and then danced all around his face.

'Yeah, but I do need to know where it came from if possible.'

'Of course, of course, come with me, we can have a

look through the back, just step round here sir, that's it,' he said. As I stepped round the counter his wife fixed me with a ferocious glare, like she was some sort of guard dog and she wanted to make it clear that if it wasn't for the presence of Tony she would have torn my throat out. I smiled politely at her and followed Tony into the store-room.

The back room of the shop was dominated by a huge terminal moraine of packaging material which threatened to engulf the shaky piles of crap-filled crates and boxes.

'Excuse the mess sir, but we don't usually have customers through here.' I felt pretty sure he could have left out the 'through here' bit, but, as he was doing me a favour, I kept my thoughts to myself.

'That's OK, can you remember where you got the, um, otter from?'

'Well, yes, as I said, I found it – quite by accident you understand – in the bottom of a case of bacon racks that I bought at an auction up in Luton, fire damaged stock . . . the boxes were a bit sooty but that was it really.'

'How did it get there?' I asked.

'That I don't know,' he replied, scanning the piles of boxes and packaging strewn around the floor, 'but maybe if we can locate the box of bacon racks it will have the manifest or the bill of lading still attached.'

With this he launched himself into one of the mounds of rubbish, tossing polystyrene, cardboard and bubble wrap aside. When he reached the bottom of the pile, he stood up and looked at me, a puzzled expression on his face; evidently the box wasn't there.

'Don't worry sir, it's somewhere round here. I opened

36

the box of bacon racks only yesterday because we sold
out the previous consignment the day before. Honestly,
I knew as soon as I saw them that I was on to a winner,
but even I'm astounded by how well they've been selling,
they're a real breakthrough.'

I'd had enough. 'Can't you just put the bacon on a
plate in the microwave?'

He stood up and looked at me aghast as if I had just
suggested we get down and dirty amongst the big, fat
maggots of polystyrene packaging on the floor. Then his
face softened, the look of horror melting to pity.

'Well you could son, but then you've got the problem
of sogginess, and, well, you might like soggy bacon, but
I can tell you for most people that's a complete no-no.'

'But couldn't you do it under the grill?' He looked at
me as if I'd just escaped from the bughouse.

'But the grill . . .' he said, almost choking on his words,
'the grill is not convenient, it's not . . . modern. With a
bacon rack and a microwave you can have the bacon
from packet to plate in under a minute, nice and crispy.
You show me the grill that'll do that for you.'

I shrugged apologetically, but Tony ignored me.

'There . . . there it is,' he said enthusiastically, his
eyes lighting up. Then he picked his way through the
rubbish to the back of the storeroom. I followed his footsteps, like we were two mountaineers crossing a
crevasse-riddled glacier.

'Yes, let's see . . . the details are usually attached in
a little plastic pocket on the outside . . . oh there we
are,' he said turning the box round for me to see, and
sure enough, there, in the middle, was a torn plastic
pocket. Unfortunately, it was empty.

'Sorry son, looks like the paperwork's missing for this one.'

Back in the shop, his wife eyed me warily.

'So, well, thanks for that, I'll just take the otter,' I said, glad to be back on the right side of the counter.

'No, problem,' said Tony, 'that'll be £49.99.'

'Whaaaa . . . fifty quid, for that?'

'No son, £49.99. After all, this is a limited edition, unique product . . . one of a kind.'

He could see I wanted it, and it was totally obvious that if I'd just wandered in and bought it straight off, he would have given it to me for like a quid or something; sorry, ninety-nine pence. I called his bluff.

'Nah mate, I didn't realise it was that much, sorry for wasting your time,' I turned and walked towards the door, hoping he would call me back. But he didn't. As I reached the door, I cracked.

'Twenty . . . I'll give you twenty quid for it,' I said, turning to face him. Tony shook his head.

'I'll take forty,' he said.

'Twenty-five?'

Tony shook his head again. 'Lowest I can go is thirty-five.'

'Thirty?'

Tony looked doubtful, then nodded, 'Deal. Thirty quid it is.'

'£29.99?'

He laughed, 'OK son, £29.99.'

I walked back to the counter, fished around in my pocket, pulled out my wallet and handed him the money. His wife slipped the statue into a wrinkled old Tesco's bag.

'Pleasure doing business with you and if you need anything else please don't hesitate to come back and see us,' said Tony brightly, smiling victoriously at his wife, who pouted sullenly, but said nothing.

'I thought this was your last day,' I said, pointing at the ENDS TODAY – EVERYTHING MUST GO' cardboard notice in the window.

Tony looked at the floor. 'Erm yes, yes, well technically speaking, it may be that we, however, make the decision to . . . extend our contract . . . or look to do some work through one of our other, ahem . . . subsidiary companies.'

I had absolutely no desire to learn any more about the murky world of Tony's retail empire, so I left the shop.

Jim was loitering against a wall next to Maccy Ds. He stood on one leg, his head bowed, his hands rammed into his pockets, straining like a motherfucker to look cool. As I approached he spotted me.

'What's in the bag?' he asked.

'Jim, tell me the truth, don't hold back on me: do I look like a Trading Standards officer?'

A look of surprise jumped onto his face and wrestled off the alienated sneer. 'Are you having flashbacks?' he asked.

When we got back to mine, I took the statue out of the bag and placed it on the breakfast bar.

'That's pretty fucked up,' said Jim, nodding thoughtfully.

'My sentiments exactly,' I replied, 'I think it's the most beautiful, fucked-up thing in this entire world.'

Jim looked at me askance. 'Hmmm,' he said sceptically.

'What do you mean, hmmm?'

'Well for a start, I'm not sure it's the most fucked-up thing . . .' said Jim.

'What is then?' I asked, a little surprised.

'Well, I once heard a story about this loser who had the money for a pair of trainers, but then went and bought some piece of obscene crap, thereby depriving himself of said trainers and bringing into question his sanity vis-à-vis the whole world. How many weeks did it take you working in Mrs P's garden to make that kind of money?'

Ever since I showed the otter statue to Jim he had been on at me about the trainers.

'Haven't you got any other money to buy them with?' he asked. I shook my head.

'What about using your mum's bank card?'

'No chance Jim, not possible.'

I won't say I wasn't tempted. Ever since I've been at school, my mother's been saving to help pay me through university, but in the last couple of years the money has doubled as a kind of emergency fund type thing which she gives me access to when she disappears on holiday. She gave me my own card for the account, along with strict instructions that I am only to use it in the event of some ill-defined serious shit. One time, last year, I tried to find out what level of seriousity the shit needed to be but she wasn't very forthcoming, though from what I could gather anything short of a full-scale nuclear attack wasn't deemed serious enough. Now, I'm not sure what good a bank card would be in those circumstances, but that's parental logic for you. And don't think she didn't check the balance and statements when she returned, because she did.

Jim picked up the otter. 'Why, Felix, why?' he asked, shaking his head.

'I want to know what it is . . .' I said, trying to order my thoughts, 'I want to know where it came from, who came up with the idea, who made it, what it means . . . look at it . . . it's a work of art.'

'Bullshit,' said Jim, who, because he's going to art college, fancies himself as a bit of an authority on the subject, 'it's not a work of art Felix; it's a piece of shit.'

I said nothing, I've learnt that it's not worth arguing with Jim about such matters.

'So you still don't know where it came from?' he asked, picking up the statue.

I shook my head.

Jim turned it over, 'There you go,' he said, handing it to me. 'China.'

I took the statue from him and looked at the base. Sure enough, stuck in the middle was a small, shiny, silver sticker with 'Product of China: Super Lucky Plastic Company Limited, Shenzhen, China' printed on it in bright red lettering.

'China,' I said thoughtfully, 'I should have guessed, everything comes from China these days.'

'Felix, would you say it was a male or female otter?' asked Jim, interrupting my thoughts.

I shrugged.

'I'd say it looks like a female otter,' said Jim.

'How come?' I asked.

'The smile, the lips, they are very . . . feminine-looking . . . actually it looks a bit like your momma.'

41

'I suppose it could be female,' I replied, ignoring the fact that he had just blatantly cussed my mother, 'but that doesn't really resolve . . . you know . . .'

'Whether he's decided to pot the pink or the brown?' asked Jim.

I nodded. It was impossible to tell; despite the detail in the rest of the statue, that precise anatomical aspect had been glossed over.

'I'm not sure it really matters, does it?' I said uncertainly.

'I don't know, is gender even a consideration when it comes to bestiality, you know, like in the eyes of the law or the church?' asked Jim.

There was a bit of a silence, whilst we both stared at the statuette and considered the legal and moral implications posed by the object in front of us.

'You have to ask yourself,' said Jim thoughtfully, 'if you actually want to meet the twisted individual who came up with this. I mean that's some pretty sick shit . . .'

'And . . .' he continued, a grin spreading slowly across his face, 'you also have to ask yourself why *you* bought this.'

'What's your point caller?' I asked, unsure what he was getting at.

'Well . . . I know you've never had much luck with the ladies . . . but I hope this doesn't mean I'm going to be reading about you in the local paper trying to explain to a judge how you were just taking a pee in this field and how you unfortunately happened to trip and fall on top of this sheep just as the police pulled up in their motor.'

*   *   *

Upstairs in my bedroom, I sat down at the computer. Jim flopped onto the bed, pulled out a packet of king-size papers and a small bag of weed and started skinning up. I swivelled round to face the screen, connected to the internet and ran a search for Shenzhen.

'Here we are . . . Shenzhen . . .' I said, reading from the screen, '. . . Shenzhen is situated in the southern coastal area of Guangdong province, 160 kilometres away from Guangzhou, and thirty-five kilometres from Hong Kong. It now has an estimated population of seven million people, though in 1978, when the city was granted Special Economic Zone status, it was a sleepy fishing port with no more than 30,000 inhabitants. It is possible to fly direct to Shenzhen, however, many business travellers choose to fly to Hong Kong and then take the one-hour train ride over the border.'

'So that's Shenzhen for you,' said Jim, after I'd finished, 'sounds pretty minging to me, I mean, what's a Special Economic Zone?'

I shrugged. 'Who knows . . . maybe I'll find out when I get there.'

Jim stopped rolling the joint and looked over at me doubtfully. 'What . . . are you trying to tell me that you're thinking of heading over to Shenzhen?'

'Not thinking Jim, I'm going . . . I really want to know what this thing is.'

'Yeah, right,' Jim said dismissively, before licking the paper and deftly sealing the joint. 'Are you totally sure you're not having flashbacks?' he continued, poking the top of the joint with a match, tamping down the weed inside.

'No, stop saying that, I swear, I never felt better, I just

43

want to know who made this thing. I want to go to Shenzhen and find out.'

'Search for it on the internet. It might save you a lot of time and money,' said Jim, ripping up an old train ticket to use as a roach.

The results for 'fat man fucks otter statue' rippled down the screen. From what I could see there were lots of porn sites, but that was about it. As I trawled through the results pages, Jim inserted the roach into the end of the spliff, inspected his handiwork and then lit it, wincing as a big lick of papery smoke ran up his face. I tried a few more permutations of 'otter' and 'fucking', but as I scanned the pages, there still seemed to be nothing of any relevance.

'Anyway, it's not even as if that statue is that hard-core,' said Jim, 'surely you can't be shocked by that thing. You've been officially desensitised.'

'How do you mean?'

'Well that otter is nowhere near as extreme as *Bad Lieutenant* or Goatse Man or even that bit in *Hannibal* where he eats that dude's brain.'

'I don't care Jim, that's not the point.'

'Then tell me Felix, what is?'

'It's not because it's shocking . . . I think it's about more than that.'

Jim cracked up. 'Yeah, right,' he snorted, 'it's just some piece of cheap porno kitsch. What do you think you'd find out in Shenzhen anyway?'

'I don't know . . . who made it and why . . . look, I don't care what you think, I'm going to Shenzhen,' I said angrily.

Jim choked on the spliff. He looked up, his eyes

watering as he tried to suppress his mirth.

'No, Jim, I'm going, tonight, if possible.'

'Yeah, yeah,' he replied, as he wiped his eyes.

'No, I *am* going,' I said furiously, massively pissed off with the way he'd just dissed the whole concept of me going to Shenzhen.

You know earlier I said that Jim was a pretty cool guy? Well you can scratch that assertion and replace it with one about him being a total dick. Jim thinks he can patronise me just because I'm a whole *year* younger and because he thinks he's cooler than shit because he's going to art college. He stared over at me. I could see he was trying to work out if I was joking. I glared back.

'How are you going to pay for it?' he asked coolly.

'The emergency bank card.'

Jim whistled. 'OK, so let me get this straight,' he said, trying to make out like he didn't understand, 'you won't use it to buy a pair of trainers, but you will use it to head off to Asia on some fucked-up wild-goose chase.'

I ignored him.

'So how much will that set you back?' he asked.

I shrugged, 'I dunno . . . I'd have to pay for the flights and a couple of nights in a cheap hotel . . . a few hundred quid, maybe.'

'And when you get back, how are you going to pay the whole thing off?'

'I should be able to pay it off from what I earn this summer.'

'What? I thought Mrs P was totally ripping you off.'

'Well, I'll get a student loan or something and pay it back from that.'

Jim leaned over and offered me the spliff. I refused. He shrugged his shoulders and took another big toke. 'Oh, come on Felix, this is your mother we're talking about here, the scariest woman in the whole of Middle Earth. I wouldn't like to be in your shoes if she found out.'

And whilst he was sneering at me in that condescending tone of his, as if I were some little kid who didn't have the wit to do anything on his own behalf, I was like, 'Fuck my mother, fuck Mrs Pretzel and fuck you too Jim.' It's hard to relate how pissed off I was. I felt totally trapped, what with my mother making me work as a slave for a mental old witch plus setting me up to jump through another set of educational hoops.

Mind you, loath as I am to admit it, Jim's implication was sort of right; I do kind of let my mother organise my life a bit too much. Take my choice of university course for example. It wasn't my idea to do a law degree; it was my mother's, but as I really have no idea what I want to do with my life I thought I'd go along with it.

Sometimes I quite fancy the idea of working in a glittering tower in a crystal city, raking in shedloads of cash. Then other days it makes me sick and it seems so clear that it's bastards like that who are fucking up the world so badly that I should do something about it, like be a protestor and live in a squat. But then it's not like that would change anything anyway. As far as I can see, all that's left for my generation to do is kill time playing PlayStation and smoking weed until the next mass extinction.

Whatever.

Within five minutes, I'd found a £500 return flight to

Hong Kong which left Heathrow at midnight, in another five minutes I'd booked it. Heathrow was just over an hour away by car. The flight took fourteen hours. Hong Kong was an hour by train from Shenzhen. I could be in Shenzhen in less than twenty-four hours. Which struck me as pretty amazing. I felt a little light-headed, like the world was suddenly full of all these possibilities.

When I finished booking the ticket I turned to find Jim lying back on my bed, blowing smoke rings into the air from a second joint he'd rolled.

'Jim, my flight leaves at midnight, you're driving me.'

'What?' said Jim sitting up, a big, stoned smile loosely affixed to his face.

'I've booked a flight to Hong Kong, it's done. I'm going.'

Jim looked at me in disbelief. 'But . . . but what about the party tonight?'

'Shit, Jim, what was I thinking . . . there's no way I want to miss catching Rob's mad scratching skillz again. I'll call the airline now and cancel the whole thing.'

Jim looked at me uncertainly and then cracked a smile. 'OK, very funny, but I still don't believe you're doing this.'

'Believe it, you're driving me to Heathrow in a couple of hours, so you'd better straighten up.'

Jim took a last draw on the joint, eyeing me carefully as he did. 'You're serious . . . aren't you?' he said as he dropped the roach into the empty Coke can on the floor, where it hissed angrily for a couple of seconds before falling silent.

*

I can see from the map on the screen that we are just about to leave mainland India behind and venture out over the Bay of Bengal. I'm still trying to figure out why I'm here.

The more I think about it the more the whole statue thing seems like an excuse. What was the real reason I did a runner? Was it the pressure of waiting for my exam results? Was it Jim's dismissive attitude? Was it the thought of working for Mrs Pretzel again? Or was it just a combination of boredom and too much weed?

Who knows? Maybe it was a mix of all of these things. I mean, have you never wanted to escape before? Just sack whatever it is you're doing and go for it?

*

Jim dropped me off at the main entrance of the airport and spun off into the night, rushing to get back to the party. Inside the terminal, I looked up at the board; there was still a couple of hours until the flight was due to take off, but the desk was open so I checked in and went straight through to the departures lounge, where I spent some time browsing the duty free and checking out all the fucked-up Eurobrands you don't get in normal shops.

A little while later I was sitting in one of the cafes, skimming through the guidebook to Hong Kong I'd just bought, when this annoying young guy in a suit sat down at the table next to me. He pushed down the retractable handle of his black trolley bag and started blahing self-importantly into his mobile to some other member of the Borg collective. I can't believe anyone would be seen in public with one of those trolley bags. They're exactly the same as the tartan shopper Mrs Pretzel uses for lugging her sherry back from the supermarket, except they're black. Mind you, I can't really speak about uncool luggage. I had my old school rucksack, which would be OK apart from the fact that it's got 'Offspring' Tippexed in massive letters across the top. Yeah, I know . . . but I was like twelve when I did it and the only other bag I've got is this massive rucksack and it would be too much hassle to drag around with me for the short time I'm going to be out there, plus I had about zero time to get my shit together. Whatever. They called the flight pretty soon after so I didn't have to suffer the Borg's empty braying too long.

On the plane, I located my seat and sat down. As I was settling in, this middle-aged guy with a shaven head stopped next to my seat. He was wearing an oversized, light-blue T-shirt tucked into a pair of baggy green jumbo cords. He was carrying a laptop bag in one hand and a nasty tan leather jacket in the other. He was so thin he looked like he'd been vacuum-packed.

'Excuse me, I think I'm sitting here,' he said, pointing to my magazines which I'd spread out on his seat. Except he said it more like, 'Excooz me, I shink I'm shitting heer,' in that totally laughable Dutch accent that Dutch people have. I picked up the magazines and wedged them in the seatback in front of me.

'Hello, I am Dennis,' he said leaning over, proffering a bony hand.

'Oh hi . . . Felix,' I said, shaking it.

Then there was this big rigmarole of him getting sorted out, folding his coat up neatly before stowing it meticulously in the overhead locker and then getting his computer out of the bag. After the whole performance was over, he sat back and cracked open the laptop. As he waited for it to boot, he launched into a little small talk.

'So what are you doing in Hong Kong?' he asked (I'll spare you the Dutch accent).

'Oh, I'm just over for a short holiday,' I answered in a non-committal type fashion. He nodded.

'And you?' I asked.

'Yes, I am on holiday too,' he replied, and he was about to say more when his laptop played a little jingle, he pointed to it apologetically and started tapping away.

About ten minutes later, the plane started to move off from the stand. A stewardess came round checking to see that our seats were in the upright position and that we were wearing our seat belts. She asked Dennis to switch off his laptop. As she did, the captain's voice came over the tannoy.

'Good evening, ladies and gentlemen, this is your captain speaking. My name is Martin Cruickshank and I, along with my co-pilot David Godfrey and the rest of the crew, would like to welcome you aboard flight WW 375 to Hong Kong. We'll be taking off in about five minutes. Meanwhile, I'd like you to listen to the safety messages from the cabin crew and I'll give you some more information about the flight shortly after we've taken off.'

He had this rich, deep, soothing voice, like a late-night DJ without the lobotomy. I reckon they must give these guys elocution lessons at pilot school, because, I don't know about you, but for me, I don't think I'd be too happy flying with a guy who had like a whiny voice or

50

a stutter or something. I looked out the window; the multi-coloured lights of the runway twinkled like rows of power ups.

I started to feel a little nervous. It's not like I hadn't flown before; I'd been to Geneva on a school skiing trip and then to Spain and France for summer holidays before my parents split up, but I'd never done a long-haul flight, so I was a bit apprehensive despite the reassuring tones of the captain. Plus, what was I doing? Jim was right, this was insane. I should stop them now, just jump up and say that I'd made a terrible mistake, and could I somehow have my money back. Dennis must have noticed my agitation.

'Are you feeling a little nervous?' he asked.

'Um, no . . . well possibly a little.'

'Do not worry, this is a very safe carrier,' he said, nodding sympathetically.

'Oh?'

'Yes, to my understanding there has only been one major accident on this carrier.'

The plane started taxiing towards the runway, and the air stewardess began that odd, bored/embarrassed safety thing, with the mad, extravagant gestures, in time to a pre-recorded tape playing over the tannoy.

'There are three emergency exits on each side of this plane. Please take a little time to familiarise yourself with their whereabouts.'

'In fact, this is also a very safe type of plane. If I remember, there are only two reported serious accidents . . . both non-fatal,' said Dennis.

I looked at him, half-trying to pay attention to what he was saying and half-trying to listen to the safety announcement. It's not like I hadn't heard the safety spiel before and I've noticed from watching other passengers in the past that it's definitely not cool to pay too much attention, or ask questions or anything . . .

Dennis piped up again. 'It is important for a rational view of such matters, though of course sometimes it is not so easy. The data can be contradictory. For example . . .'

'In the unlikely event of a landing in water you will find life jackets stowed under the seat in front of you.'

'. . . there is a commonly held perception that the drive to the airport is, in fact, more dangerous than your subsequent flight . . .'

'Cabin doors and cross-check.'

'. . . however, a study from the US refutes this notion. During the year of study, it was calculated that fifty billion miles were travelled on commercial flights, during the course of which 580 people lost their lives; giving a death rate of, if I can remember correctly . . . about eleven deaths per billion air miles travelled.'

'Cabin crew, seats ready for take-off.' The plane swung round onto the end of the runway, the engines, which had been purring away quietly as we taxied from the terminal, burst into a throaty roar.

'Now compare this with car travel,' said Dennis, raising his voice over the increased engine noise, 'where in the same year an estimated 37,000 people died on the US roads and an estimated 4750 billion miles were travelled, giving a death rate of about seven deaths per billion miles travelled – significantly less than air travel.'

As the plane accelerated down the runway, it began

to shake. It felt heavy and sluggish, like a bus with wings. I started to feel a little sick.

'Anyway, it's only take-off and landing that you have to worry about. Over eighty per cent of accidents happen during these two phases of flight,' concluded Dennis as the plane skipped lightly off the ground and into the air. As we climbed steeply into the dark night, I looked down on the spider's web of orange street lights below.

'Where are you headed in Hong Kong?' I asked, trying to divert the conversation away from the whole area of air travel fatalities.

'Chep Lap Kok airport,' replied Dennis.

'Yeah, but after?' I asked, grabbing hold of the armrests of my seat as the plane banked sharply to the left.

'No, that's where I'm staying.'

'What do you mean, I thought you were going on a holiday?'

'I am, I'm a plane spotter.'

'A plane spotter?'

'Yes, I'm interested in planes. Chep Lap Kok is a great airport, one of the major world hubs. It has been voted World Airport of the Year three times in a row.'

'You're not pulling my leg are you?' I asked, forgetting he was Dutch.

'Pulling your leg?' he repeated, frowning.

'Oh yeah, sorry, it's slang for joking.'

'Heh, heh,' he laughed softly, his face cracking into a big, cheesy, Edam grin. 'That's pretty funny. In the Netherlands we would say pulling your nose.'

The plane began to level out; the coiled spring in my gut loosened a little. The voice of the captain came over the tannoy again. 'I'd like to welcome you again onto flight WW 375 to Hong Kong, we got off the ground on schedule, so if you'd just like to keep your seat belts fastened for a few minutes more until I extinguish the fasten seat belts sign, sit back, relax and enjoy your flight with us tonight. Flight time is about fourteen hours, depending on the prevailing winds, but I'll update you with our progress as we continue.'

'So what's safer; driving to the airport or flying?' I asked after the captain had finished.

'That depends on who you believe,' said Dennis.

'Who do you believe?' I asked.

'That doesn't matter so much I think as who do you believe,' he replied, smiling enigmatically.

I must have looked concerned again, because Dennis hit me with some more statistics.

'Look, in case you're still worried, Felix, I will relay to you one last piece of information: there was another study done in the US which surveyed a period of almost ten years. This study found that the mortality risk per person, per flight for international jet travel in the Western world was one in five million.' I shrugged, trying to work out what this actually meant. Dennis, to give him his due, had his shit down cold.

'What this means Felix, is that if you took a flight every day for 13,000 years you would be involved in one fatal crash – you divide the five million by 365 days . . . to put that in perspective, 13,000 years ago humans were still living in caves and hunting with sticks and stones.' I settled back in my seat, feeling a little more relaxed.

'Of course, you should remember that however remote the odds, you are as likely to crash today as you

54

are at any other point in those 13,000 years,' said Dennis.

A cute stewardess walked by. Dennis stopped her. 'Excuse me miss, could you tell me what the vegetarian option is tonight?'

HONG KONG

It's 6.00 a.m. Hong Kong time. I was woken about half an hour ago by the air-con unit in my room wheezing away like some bronchial pervert engaged in a particularly tight game of pocket billiards. I reached over and switched it off, but then it started to get really hot and sweaty so I switched it on again. But then I couldn't get back to sleep for the noise.

As I lay there in the pitch black, windowless room, listening to the asthmatic air-con, I started to get the weirdest feeling. It was like I could sense the malevolent presence of the statue, as if the man and the otter were alive, quietly fucking in the dark. The whole thing was totally disturbing, kind of like imagining your parents having sex but much worse. In the end I got so freaked out that I switched on the light, opened the bag, pulled out the statue and placed it on the bed in front of me. In the harsh glare of the fluorescent strip light the statue seemed harmless. I was just being stupid. I was obviously jet-lagged or something. I put it back in the bag and decided to update this diary.

We landed last night at about 10.00 p.m. Hong Kong time and as soon as we did Dennis leaned over me and peered out the window, scanning around for planes to spot.

'Look Felix, a Boeing 707, in Emirates livery. I am sure this is an aircraft I have previously spotted in Dallas, Texas.'

For quite a serious-minded, oldish geezer he definitely came across a bit like a little kid, I mean, he was so pleased when he saw the Emirates 707, I thought he was going to offer to high-five me. But he didn't, he just pulled out a little, black notebook and jotted down the details of the plane.

As Dennis and I went through immigration and customs together I got a bit nervous again, not that I had any reason to, but I don't know, I had this bad feeling that maybe someone had stuffed my bag full of drugs as part of a plot with a corrupt customs official or something. I started to get these visions of me banged up in a bamboo cage in some squalid prison, like one of those tragic, emaciated motherfuckers from good homes in Surrey or wherever that you see on the news. The ones who claim that despite the fact that the author-ities found six kilos of smack stuffed up their poop-shoots, they are totally innocent and were duped into doing it by someone else. You know, the ones whose parents you see making televised appeals for clemency to whatever government, with the mum sniffling into a handkerchief and the dad being the strong one and answering most of the questions with his arm clamped round his wife as they face the cameras in front of their suburban semi with the little patches of moss on the roof. The suburban semi which has the Labrador shut in the kitchen on account of the press being there and the utility room that has a neat, freshly laundered pile of their little darling's summer clothes that mum is going to parcel up and send after the press has gone . . .

Whatever.

In the event all I got was a brief glare from the official as she compared me with my photo. Then she stamped my passport, handed it back to me and waved me on. I looked at the stamp as I walked through customs. It was pretty cool, I mean, you don't get stamps for going to France and Spain which meant that it was the first one in my passport; it made me feel like I was a real traveller. As I was inspecting my passport Dennis caught up with me, he was carrying his passport too. It was huge, like, it was almost the size of the novels that you get in airport bookshops, you know, the ones with embossed covers which the Borg like to read on planes and pretend that they too are engaged in international espionage, instead of actually selling dishwashers or whatever.

Dennis spotted that I was scoping his passport.

'Special issue,' he said with a hint of pride in his voice, before handing it to me. I flipped through it. It was crammed full of different stamps and visas. 'I think I have been in over seventy countries in the last three years,' he said, beaming at me. All of which made me feel a little less like an international jet-setter.

Once we were through the gate, Dennis stopped and shook my hand. 'Well, Felix, it was very nice to meet you. I hope you enjoy your time in Hong Kong.'

'Yeah . . . and you, I hope you . . . er, have good luck with the planes.'

Dennis smiled, then turned and headed off in the direction of the observation deck for some hardcore, late night plane spotting.

I looked around. Dennis was right about Chep Lap Kok, it was impressive. A big, airy cathedral of glass and steel. Somehow, however, it didn't really seem that foreign. All the shops were pretty much the same as in Heathrow, and the people didn't look that different. I found it hard to believe that I was now halfway around the world. Part of me felt that we could have been flying around in circles above South-East England for fourteen hours before landing again.

I sat down on one of the brushed steel benches, opened my guidebook and flicked to the budget part of the accommodation section. After a little consideration, I selected the second cheapest hostel listed. It was called the Blue Lotus and it was on Nathan Road.

By the time the metro arrived at Nathan Road I totally expected the whole place to be deserted. I was wrong. It was around 11.30 in the evening when I stepped out into a great river of people all bathed in the dazzling light from a million neon signs which ran up the sides of the tower blocks lining the street, like some garish coral reef blazing away in the muggy heat of the night. I just stood and gawped for a couple of minutes. It was hot. A trickle of sweat gathered between my shoulder blades and slithered down my spine.

I shrugged off my rucksack, pulled out my guidebook and looked at the map, but it seemed to make no sense. A couple of people bumped into me so I stepped back towards the wall of the station, a sickly, sweet-and-sour smell seeped up from a drain at my feet. I started to feel a little overwhelmed.

'You want a suit sir?'

I looked up from the guidebook. In front of me stood this Sikh geezer. He was wearing a neat, black turban; his beard tied up with a little net.

'Erm . . .' I replied hesitantly, I mean, who buys a suit at midnight? It was clearly some sort of tactic.

'Best price in town boss, best quality too, all hand stitched,' he said, stepping forward and offering me a flyer.

'Er, no, sorry,' I was totally wary. He'd obviously spotted me as being fresh off the boat and now he was going to try and lure me into his shop, where I'd be drugged and then bummed or something.

'Maybe tomorrow boss?' he said, virtually thrusting the flyer into my hand.

'Maybe,' I said.

'Where you stay?' he asked.

'Blue Lotus Guest House . . . but I can't find it,' I replied without thinking.

'Oh, yes, boss, it's over the street . . . see that apartment block there, it's got a sign . . . I think it's on the seventeenth floor.'

'Oh, thanks,' I replied, grateful that he had shown me where it was, but also sort of regretting having told him. Now he knew where I was going to be staying. Maybe he was even in league with the owner of the Blue Lotus, maybe he had a henchman up there who would cosh me and then I'd wake up in a set of stainless steel stocks and there'd be this big, sweaty German in a gimp suit with a huge buzz-bomb in his hand . . .

63

These things happen. You've seen the stories in the Sunday papers, right? The ones about these kids from nice homes in Surrey or wherever and their 'THREE YEARS OF HELL IN ASIAN SEX DUNGEON'. About how they were on this back-packing trip during their 'hols from uni' or whatever and how they met this friendly guy/girl/ladyboy in a bar and how they'd only had a couple of drinks, but suddenly they felt really wasted, and then when they woke up . . .

Whatever.

I thanked the Sikh guy and crossed the road. Outside the entrance to the tower block, I hesitated and looked round. He was still standing there. He returned my stare with a big thumbs up. He couldn't be in league, surely . . . it would be too big of a coincidence. Plus, I felt totally shit, like an empty can full of fag butts and roaches all soaked in the spitty dregs of Coke. An ambulance screamed past, driving right through my skull on its way to wherever. I put my qualms to one side, pushed open the doors and caught the lift to the seventeenth floor.

OK, I know all of this sounds a little paranoid, but I guess I was feeling a bit freaked out from the flight and being in a foreign country. When I've been abroad before it's mainly been with my parents or school and, you know, it's a little like a bubble, where everything's been sorted out beforehand.

The one time I did spend any time on my own in a foreign country was pretty traumatic, in fact, I'd say it was like the worst month of my life.

Two summers ago my mother signed me up for this French exchange trip. I didn't want to go, but she insisted.

Basically, I was totally marooned in this desolate little village in the South of France with a family that completely ignored me. They just carried on with their lives as if I didn't exist. Most of the time I was left at the house, and because it was way out in the sticks and there was very little public transport, it meant I couldn't even escape the place. I spent a lot of time just sitting around watching French television, which, by the way, totally blows. Seriously, I'd prefer to end up in an Asian sex dungeon than sit through another French chat show interview with Jane Birkin or Johnny Halliday or whoever.

But that wasn't the worst, because, in addition to the boredom, I was also getting bullied senseless by Jean Pierre, the co-exchangee or whatever the fuck you call them, and there was nothing I could do about it.

Because I'd been put forward a year at school, on account of my enormous intellect, Jean Pierre was a year older than me. Plus, I've never been a big kid for my age and he was one of the forwards in his school rugby team, so he was about twice my size. I was totally at his mercy, of which, it quickly transpired, he had none. When his parents weren't around he spent his whole time punching me in the guts and giving me wedgies and dead legs; all sorts of twisted shit. I couldn't even speak French well enough to grass him up, I mean, what is the French for 'Your son just gave me a nipple cripple'? And anyway, I totally doubt his parents would have:

(a)   believed me; or
(b)   given a shit.

As far as his mother was concerned, Jean Pierre was some kind of reincarnation of the little baby Jesus, an opinion that even she might have had occasion to revise if she knew what the disgusting bastard did to me every morning. The first time it happened I had no idea what was going on, I woke to find that I was being semi-suffocated by something warm and heavy pressing down on my face. I started to panic, struggling to escape, but I was pinned down. Just when I thought I was going to pass out, suddenly the weight lifted, Jean Pierre ripped off and jumped free. I gasped like a motherfucker on account of the suffocation and inhaled a lungful of his foul, frog arse gas.

As I was coughing and spluttering and trying not to puke, he did a little bow and said 'Good morning Britain,' in his horrible French accent. Virtually every day for a month he woke me by farting on my head, and there was nothing I could do, there was no lock on my door and he was always up before me to go rugby training. I'd never much liked rugby before that, having being forced to play it in my younger days at school, but Jean Pierre's involvement sealed my hatred for that so-called sport, if in fact you can call it a sport, because as far as I can see it's just an excuse for men to give each other rough cuddles in the mud and then get in the bath together. Now, I'm as liberal as the next person about such matters, it's just that I think they should come out in the open about it, you know, denial can be very psychologically detrimental in the long term.

Whatever.

When I got home I swore never to set foot on French soil again. Unfortunately, that was not the end of Jean

Pierre, it being an exchange visit and everything. When he came over to the UK the next month, I was prepared for similar treatment. He was massively pleasant to my mother at the airport, acting like he was the little baby Jesus again and of course she totally loved him. But when we were left alone, to my surprise and relief, he didn't beat me up, he just ignored me, because, get this: he was too busy fingering like every single girl in the neighbourhood to have any time to bully me. I swear, all the girls totally fell for him, just because he had a six-pack. Girls who hadn't even got off with any of the guys at school suddenly dropped their knickers in the most flagrant manner. It was totally sordid.

I eventually found the door to the Blue Lotus down a maze of corridors, deep in the belly of the building. Screwed to the wall at the side of the door, above a grubby intercom unit, were three brass plaques, one for the Blue Lotus Hostel, one for the Blue Lotus Travel Agency and one for the Blue Lotus Import/Export Agency.

I pressed the buzzer and then tried to peer through the frosted reinforced glass window set in the door.

'What you want?' asked a woman over the intercom.

'Oh, yeah, hi, I'm looking for a room,' I said leaning in towards it.

'How many nights?'

'One . . . maybe two.'

'I need see passport, show at window,' she said.

I rummaged in my bag, opened the passport and pressed it flat against the glass. A blurry face appeared on the other side. After a short pause, there was a low buzz and the door swung open.

The Blue Lotus was not what I expected. It was advertised as a hostel in the guidebook and I was kind of anticipating ping-pong tables and lots of jovial young people with backpacks and whatever; instead I seemed to be standing in someone's kitchen.

It was pretty basic, a couple of woks hung on the back wall above a greasy cooker set in between chipped blue formica units piled high with papers and other junk.

'Hello, my name is Miss Frances,' said the woman at the door in slightly halting English, 'and this is my mother,' she said, pointing to this withered old crone sitting on a small stool next to a huge mound of purple, spiky, alien fruit. Her mother flashed me a big, toothless smile, picked up a piece of the fruit which she peeled and tossed into a big, black plastic dustbin sitting next to her.

The whole scenario did nothing to allay my fears that Miss Frances was some kind of black widow type individual who had a deal with the Sikh guy downstairs. Maybe, I thought, her import/export business dealt in human organs or something. Maybe they'd kill me in my sleep, remove the valuable bits like my heart and kidneys, and then get the old lady to chop the rest of me up into a big, black bucket which they'd sell for fish bait or dog food . . .

'You come with me,' said Miss Frances, before walking towards a door at the back of the room. I hesitated for a second, but then I looked at her and felt foolish. She was about half my size and her mother was even smaller. What could they do?

The room was tiny, about the same size as one of my mother's walk-in wardrobes. It was empty apart from a rickety bunk bed and a decrepit air-con unit which was attached to the back wall with grey duct tape. As I looked over at the bunk bed, I was almost knocked off my feet by a massive tidal wave of nostalgia. The cover sheet on the bottom bunk was the exact same as the duvet cover I'd had when I was a kid. It was a *Power Rangers* one, or to be more precise, it had Jason, ex-leader of the Red Rangers, on it. He had his Power Sword in one hand (no giggling at the back) and the Tyrannosaurus Coin in the other. Jason was like the ultimate Ranger, until of course he left and joined the World Teen Summit at a peace conference in Switzerland.

The sheet was a bit faded, but *Power Rangers*; I loved that programme. Me and my Computer Club mate Kevin were pretty obsessed with it for a while, always trying to outdo each other with our arcane knowledge. Usually it ended up in these massive arguments about the stories. For example, I remember one time where we had this huge battle about an episode where Zordon released an energy wave which supposedly cleansed the whole universe of evil, but then, in the next episode, the universe was back to normal and there were all these evil beings again. To begin with neither of us could understand that, and they made totally no mention of it either, as if it had never happened. So I said it must just have been a tempo-rary effect, but Kevin disagreed and argued that Zordon only *claimed* that he had cleansed the whole universe of evil, but in fact he knew it was only an illusion. OK, I don't want to rehash the whole thing here, but that was such a specious claim. There was no way that Zordon was an unreliable narrator . . . when he said he'd do something, he did it. I'll concede that it was possible that he could have *thought* he'd cleansed the universe of evil, but was genuinely mistaken, but that's not what Kevin was arguing.

Whatever.

I don't want you to think that I still have the *Power Ranger* duvet cover at home or anything. I got rid of that stuff a long time ago, it's just that it was quite a big coincidence and I was feeling a little freaked out at the thought that I might be slopping around in a big, black plastic bucket in the morning.

'I show you shower,' said Miss Frances, interrupting my thoughts.

The shower room was opposite. It was long and narrow, with a toilet at one end and a shower in the middle, but there was no cubicle or anything. Another big black bucket, this time full of fat, wormy noodles, stood next to the shower.

Miss Frances saw me eyeing the bucket: 'Don't worry, I move it for tonight. It for big church meal tomorrow.' She pointed at a wall calendar in the corridor behind us, which had a picture of a small whitewashed church hall surrounded by skyscrapers. 'Lutheran Church of Hong Kong' was printed across the bottom of the calendar in bright red lettering. It did a lot to put my mind at rest about the whole organ-smuggling thing.

We stepped back into the kitchen.

'Is OK?' asked Miss Frances, smiling.

'Yeah, great. I'll take it.' As I said, the place was not quite what I'd expected, but she seemed friendly enough, and I felt far too tired to trog around town looking for somewhere else.

'How long you stay?' she asked again.

70

'I think just one night . . . but maybe two,' I replied.

'Where you go after?'

'Shenzhen.'

'How you get there?'

I shrugged.

'You get train, five-day visa at border,' she said emphatically.

'You need visa?' I asked.

'Yes, most time you need special visa for China, but for Shenzhen, no problem. They stamp when you cross over, no need to apply at embassy.'

'OK . . . I need book train tickets also?' I replied, noticing that for some fucked-up reason, I had started dropping all the conjunctions from my speech.

'No worry,' she said looking at her watch, 'I can get.'

'Now?'

'Sure, no problem,' she smiled, 'Blue Lotus Travel Agency.'

'You want me pay now?'

'No, no, no,' she said, 'I trust you. You are very good-looking young man.'

I blushed. 'Er, thank you. When you think they ready?'

She looked up at a large clock above the fridge. 'I think maybe if lucky, I get tickets tonight, maybe you can leave tomorrow morning, no worry though, I will make sure it happen.'

Back in the room I dumped my rucksack on the top bunk and lay down on the bottom one. It was pretty nice to stretch out after the plane journey, but though my body felt tired, my mind was still buzzing with the events of the last couple of days. I didn't feel like sleeping.

As I lay and tried to chill out, there was a knock on the door. It was Miss Frances.

'Felix,' she said loudly, so as to be heard through the door, 'train tickets booked, ready for you tomorrow morning, train leave 1.00 p.m.'

Which was a total result. I jumped up, opened the door and thanked her, she smiled and then, as she turned to head back into the kitchen, I remembered that I needed to check my e-mail.

'Oh, yeah, sorry to . . . is there anywhere I can check internet?'

Miss Frances nodded. 'Out on Nathan Road, many internet cafes. Look for sign.'

Even though it was around midnight crowds still packed the pavements, though it all seemed a bit more manageable since I had a place to stay and I'd dropped off my rucksack. The Sikh dude was still hanging around outside the tube station. He saw me and waved. I hesitated and then waved back, before plunging into the crowd. For a little while I just walked randomly, taking in the new sights and sounds, scoping out the big electronics shops, the tailors, the jewellers, the snack stalls and juice bars. Pretty soon I spotted a big sign for an internet cafe over a narrow doorway next to a small shop selling DVDs and VCDs. A set of grubby stairs, covered in flyers for bands and club nights, led down to a basement. As I headed down them, I was met by the chatter of automatic gunfire, rocket explosions and the hideous screams of the dead and dying, all mashed up with some totally banging, nosebleed techno playing over the cafe PA.

The place was packed with cool-looking kids, all smoking like motherfuckers and playing an assortment of networked fragfests. I got a pass number from a bored, cute-looking girl with pink hair extensions who sat behind the counter drinking a can of Diet Coke.

When I opened my webmail there were two messages: one from Jim and one from my mother. My heart skipped a beat, I was like, 'Shit, has she found out or something?'

I opened my mother's mail first.

RE: RE: Instructions for Holiday
Felix,
Sandra and I arrived safely in Newark two days ago. We drove to Vermont yesterday. Today was great fun, we went hiking in the backwoods with a guide and a nice young couple from Des Moines (Iowa) called Shawn and Tracey. I'm in the hotel internet cafe just now and we're all due to meet for dinner in about ten minutes, so I'll be brief.
Dora has been in touch and informs me that you are not working at the moment as her mother-in-law's dog is unwell. I want to impress on you that you will have to return to work for Mrs Pretzel as soon as the dog recovers. Apparently it is still 'touch and go', however, according to Dora it should be resolved one way or another in the next couple of days.

I would like to make it clear that whatever the outcome, you **will** be returning to work at that point. If the dog has died, then I expect you to be extra helpful and sympathetic. Dora also informs me that she phoned you with this information yesterday, and left a message on the machine, as you didn't answer. I sincerely hope that you are not up to something, because be assured, if you are, I **will** find out and the consequences **will not** be pleasant.

You must remember that you are going to university soon and whilst you are there you will have to take a much more responsible view of the world or you will find yourself left behind. Your three years there are the most important of your life, and you will have to pull your socks up if you are going to achieve your full potential. OK, I've just seen Sandra walk into the lobby, so I'll have to go. In the meantime, if you are up to something stop it immediately.

    Love,
    Mum

Fuck. Like in one short e-mail there were about fifteen million different issues, which are hard to understand unless you've met my mother.

My mother is a short, energetic woman who spends her whole life in the middle of this whirlwind of business meetings, charity fundraisers and hairspray. Employment-wise, she's like the PA for the boss of some company that makes software that tracks the number of pens in a company or something and then spits out reports so other companies can keep a firm hold of their pen situations and make sure they don't have too many red pens, as opposed to blue or black ones. It's a little weird if you ask me, spending your life working for a company that makes a piece of software that tracks the movements of pens in a company. I tried to point this out one time. Big fucking mistake. I had no idea she took the thing so seriously, like totally, and she went on and on about who do you think pays for this, and how I don't know I'm born, and how I should grow up and realise the sacrifices she's had to make. Then she started on about the real world. At which point I totally switched off. If there's one thing I hate, it's people crapping on about the real world, like somehow they're the only people who actually live in the real world and you, or whoever they are taking to task about whatever, don't. And another thing, the real world to which they refer is always a shithole. Like they *never* say c'mon, live in the real world, it's a great place, full of lovely people, with some great beaches and some really tasty food. No, it's always like, live in the real world, it's absolutely shit and you're fooling yourself if you think otherwise.

Plus, what was all that stuff in the e-mail about the next three years of my life being the most important? What about my 'A' Levels? Two years ago I was told that the next two years were going to be the most important of my life. Now suddenly the next three years are the most important. I'm beginning to see a pattern forming here.

Of course, maybe she's right and it's all important. Mind you, I think she still has aspirations about me being prime minister one day.

Don't get me wrong, it's been pretty hard for my mother since the divorce, what with having to look after two kids on her own and hold down a job. It's just that sometimes I think she's maybe a little too harsh on me. I mean, it's not like the divorce didn't hit me and my sister hard as well. Sometimes I think my mother should lighten up a bit.

Whatever.

I sent her a reply assuring her I was not up to anything and that yes, I would be able to resume working for Mrs Pretzel whenever I got the call.

The e-mail from Jim asked how I was and recounted his exploits at Jessica's party. I'll spare you the details.

As I replied to his mail I suddenly started to feel pretty exhausted, all I wanted to do was sleep and I think I could have despite the sickening scream and crunch of a chainsaw ripping through zombie flesh coming from the terminal next to me. I looked at my watch. It was just before 1.00 a.m. Hong Kong time, which meant that it was 5.00 p.m. back home. If I'd still been working for Mrs Pretzel I'd have been finishing up for the day.

*

Typically I'd pitch up at Mrs P's at around 9.00 a.m. and work in the garden for a couple of hours with Mrs P directing operations from the patio. She'd be like, 'Felix, be careful to avoid the poinsettia, it was a present from Clarice . . . Felix you shouldn't dig with your lower back,

76

stand more upright . . . Felix, you missed some nettles
. . . there just to the right . . .'

Generally speaking, I ignored her, spending most of
my time indiscriminately hacking the shit out of anything
that crossed my path. OK, I know, but if she wanted a
decent job doing she should have hired a professional,
or at least paid me what I was due.

After a couple of hours of hand-to-hand combat with
assorted vegetation, I'd take a break and we'd play a
game of Scrabble. Seriously. It started on my very first
day; she called me up to the house at about 11.00, on
the patio table was a cup of tea, a Scrabble board and
a battered old dictionary.

'Do you play?' she asked, nodding in the direction of
the board. I shrugged. I mean, I'd played a bit with my
family when I was younger, but that was before my
parents got divorced. 'It is very beneficial for your vocab-
ulary,' she continued airily, 'and an extensive vocabu-
lary is an invaluable tool in this life. My late husband
Aubrey used to say that all a man needs to get on in this
world are good manners, a good tailor and a good vocab-
ulary.'

So we played Scrabble every day. I wasn't complaining,
it was better than having to work.

The first time we played she totally thrashed me.
Mainly because she kept coming up with these obscure
little words, stuff like 'ama' and 'zho' that she always
somehow managed to get onto triple word scores and
shit. Words that I doubt even Aubrey used in his everyday
life, unless of course he had regular dealings with
Japanese pearl divers or Tibetan yak herders.

As we cleared the pieces away she couldn't help but

gloat. 'Which university are you going to Felix?' she asked, smiling. I have since learnt that it is always a bad sign when she smiles.

'Cambridge,' I replied tentatively.

'Oh, yes,' she said in a rather dismissive tone, 'of course I never went to university, in my day it wasn't the done thing for *nice* girls.'

I was like, 'So what was stopping *you* then?'

'Yes, I think university is all very well for a certain type of person, but frankly it strikes me as a terrible waste of time. Aubrey never went to university and he had a very successful career in business.'

'What did Aubrey do?' I asked.

'He was a successful businessman,' she replied, blocking my attempted passing shot down the line with her sliced backhand.

'What kind of business?' I asked, trying to lob her.

'Felix, I've run out of cigarettes. Would you be a darling and run off and get me a pack?' she said, rising on her tiptoes and smashing a winner from my underplayed lob.

Seriously, she really doesn't like talking about Aubrey. Every time I try and find out anything about him, I get the stonewall treatment.

Anyway, after she kicked my ass at Scrabble I'd usually do a bit more gardening while she polished off the remainder of the sherry. Then, when she was good and pissed, she'd stagger off for a catnap, only to reappear around three-ish in a totally foul mood. Then she'd boss me around some more before wobbling off down to the bank and shops with her tartan trolley bag in tow.

Apparently, she goes to the bank every day and checks her balance to make sure they're not cheating her. She told me that they tried to get her to use the cash machines but she refused and threatened to withdraw her money. So they caved in to her. Un-fucking-believable.

I also discovered that the reason she waits around until later in the day to do her shopping is because that's when she can buy all the reduced shit on the cheap, like all these fell meats and bruised fruit and bashed tins or whatever. Her diet is completely random, and totally disgusting, and I wouldn't have minded so much if she hadn't tried to make me eat the stuff as well. One time she came back with this huge, out of date pie, which had mould growing on one corner. I got out of eating it by saying it was against my religion to eat pies, but a couple of days later she scored a big box of these minging apples. She insisted I had one, and there was no way I could get out of it. I tried to refuse but she wouldn't let it go. In the end I took a bite of one to get her off my back, but as soon as she wasn't looking I spat it out and flung the rest of the apple into the bushes, which of course set Vespasian chasing after it, woofing like a motherfucker.

*

After I finished my e-mails I made my way back to the Blue Lotus. Miss Frances answered the door and let me in.

'Ah, Felix good to see you, it all fixed, I give you ticket tomorrow morning,' she said smiling. She turned to leave when I remembered that I needed to get some money out.

'Oh, sorry . . . how do I get money for China?' I asked.

'You have plastic?' she asked. I nodded.

'It OK for Shenzhen. Use cash machine there like here.'

'You sure?'

'Yes, no problem.'

All of which came as a bit of a surprise. Sometimes you've got to be totally impressed. With one little piece of plastic I could access money almost anywhere in the world, even communist China.

As I said earlier on, despite being tired I slept badly. As I sat on my bunk and updated this diary, I thought about my next step. I realised that I had no idea about what I was going to do when I got to China. In fact, despite the fact that I did History 'A' Level, I realised that I didn't even know anything about China. The most populous country in the world, with an illustrious history stretching back millennia and I knew virtually nothing about it, except what I'd gleaned from a few old-skool Shaolin flicks.

Anyway, it's 8.00 a.m now so I'm going to have some breakfast and then see if I can get a haircut, because it did occur to me that, assuming I can get to see them, it's probably better that I don't turn up at the door of Super Lucky Plastic Company Limited looking like a young Keith Richards, or even a Trading Standards officer for that matter.

SHENZHEN

I stood watching the dumpy white Star ferries plough their way doggedly across the narrow channel between Kowloon and the glittering bar graph of skyscrapers on Hong Kong Island. I pushed back my 'I Love Hong Kong' baseball cap and scratched my head, which was still itchy from the haircut I'd just got. I was killing time before my train left.

It had taken me a while to find a decent-looking hairdresser. The one I went for in the end had all these cool pictures of models in the front window sporting a range of hairdos, from complex razor cuts and mohawks to mullets and mad-arsed raver dos with purple and orange extensions. Not that I was looking to get a radical cut, I just wanted something presentable, but not too uncool, so that after my meeting with Super Lucky Plastic Company Limited I could spike it up a little and not look like a complete tool.

The hairdresser's was empty apart from these three guys sitting around playing guitars and smoking cigarettes. I was a little taken aback, but the place looked pretty professional. It had all the proper, fucked-up backwards sinks, plus the three guys had supercool hairdos, like the ones in the pictures in the window. When I asked them about a haircut, they looked at each other blankly for a bit without saying anything, then one of them got up with a weary look on his face and pointed to one of the chairs.

The dude that cut my hair gave me a style book to look at and I picked out this quite cool short do, which I could have passed off as being sensible if I wanted. But when he finished and I checked it in the mirror, it looked nothing like the hairdo in the book. I don't know if it was deliberate, but I swear it's the worst haircut I've ever had in my entire life. I don't even know how to begin to describe it, though if you can picture how a gorilla's hair is, like really short at the front and sort of piled up in a tufty pyramid on top, and then if you can imagine that the same gorilla had just undergone an intensive course of chemotherapy, then you're not too far away. When I tried to explain that it wasn't what I wanted, I got the same blank kind of look as before. What could I do? I suppose I could have refused to pay them, but they looked pretty mean.

As I walked out the shop I'm sure I heard the bastards sniggering.

That's why I was wearing the 'I Love Hong Kong' baseball cap. It covered up the worst of the damage and I thought it was just about naff enough to be cool in an ironic kind of way. Whatever. It was a hundred million times better than my monkey-man hairdo.

As the train pulled out of Hung Hom station it started to rain gently. I looked through the windows, watching as the high-rise city dissolved into acid green rice paddies.

84

After about half-an-hour buildings started to sprout again from the fertile earth and fifteen minutes later we came to a juddering halt at Lo Wu, the stop at the border. Then there was a massive rush as everyone on the train jumped up and headed down the platform; I followed. It took about an hour to get through customs and immigration and then suddenly I was in China. OK, I know Hong Kong is officially part of China these days, but it's different.

The first thing I noticed when I stepped out of the station was this big, glass and steel shopping mall flanked by serried ranks of shimmering skyscrapers, much like those in Hong Kong. More than half of the people from the train seemed to be heading towards the mall. I was a bit taken aback. I'd sort of expected something on a bit more of a communist tip, like with lots of bicycles and possibly even a few tanks. Instead, it seemed that Shenzhen was just another retail opportunity.

However, I did spot some immediately obvious differences. For example, a pair of women wearing green uniforms with red trim standing at the exit of the station. They looked very official, but oddly one of them was wearing a pair of beaten up old Nikes. Plus, it was clear that most of the people were less cool and generally poorer than the people in Hong Kong.

As I stood taking all of this in, a guy with an unruly rick of thick black hair sidled up to me, reached into his jacket and pulled out a carton of cigarettes. I tried to wave him away, but he just stood there and kept trying to hand me the cigarettes while he crapped away in Chinese. I pulled out my guidebook and tried to ignore him. As I did, this dodgy-looking big dude in a grubby brown suit pushed the cigarette seller aside.

'Taxi,' he said gruffly.

I shook my head. He spat on the floor. It was totally gross.

'Taxi,' he said again, grabbing my sleeve and tugging it insistently.

'No, I no want,' I replied, shaking free of his grip. He stared at me. Then, from behind me, I heard this other voice.

'Mattress Relo, Hairy Pot.' I looked round to find a youngish dude wearing a white, short-sleeved shirt, holding up this fan of pirated DVDs; ripped discs, with shitty, photocopied covers.

'You buy?' he said, holding the DVDs out to me like he was a magician who wanted me to pick a card, any card.

'No, no want anything,' I said, shaking my head. The big taxi geezer stepped forward and pushed the DVD seller to one side then grabbed my arm again. I could feel my stomach tightening. I stood there grinning like a motherfucker. I suddenly felt terribly alone. I was in a foreign country, where the rules were different, the language was different. The big man tugged my arm again. It was so hot, my back was clammy with sweat, my neck itched from the haircut.

'Taxi?'

'OK, so you know one word of English,' I said, losing my temper a little. I looked up at the departures board and saw that there was a train leaving every thirty minutes. I could be back in Hong Kong in a couple of hours. It was weird, like now Hong Kong, which only twenty-four hours before had seemed odd and alien, felt like home.

Anyway, just as I was thinking about maybe heading back to Hong Kong, I heard a voice calling in English.

'Mister, mister.'

I looked down from the board and spotted this kid walking over the station concourse in my direction. He was smaller than me, dressed in an LA Lakers T-shirt, these totally half-mast combat trousers, and a pair of heavily scuffed, slip on, patent leather loafers. Not a good look.

'Hey mister, you need hotel?' he said, waving as he trotted towards me.

'You speak English?' I asked over the crowd.

'Yeah, I speak English real good,' he replied with this big American drawl, like he was some Texan oil baron, 'where you from?'

'I'm British.'

'Ah, David Beckham, he is the best footballer in the world, no?' the drawl suddenly gone.

'Yeah, yeah,' I said, like I knew him personally, so pleased was I to meet someone that spoke English.

'You need hotel?'

'Yeah sure, but not expensive.'

'No problem. You traveller?'

'No, not really. I'm here on business.'

'Business . . . you need interpreter?'

'Uh, maybe.'

As we walked down the street I felt calmer. I looked back at the station, the DVD seller stood staring vacantly in our direction.

'My name is Cheng, what is yours?'

'Felix . . . my name is Felix,' I replied, turning back to face my new companion.

'Felix,' he said, taking it for a test drive. Like, I'm not going to go into the whole R and L thing here, but he did have some trouble, but then it's not like I can speak a single word of Chinese, let alone pronounce the mother-fucking language.

'Yes, Felix, not to trust taxi drivers at station, they are all thieves, they all overcharge, no good,' he said shaking his head vigorously to show the strength of his dislike for such people. All very well I thought, but why should I trust you?

'You no need taxi for hotel anyway, only short walk to hotel, fifty US dollars per night get you very nice hotel, one hundred US dollars get you five-star luxury. Plenty hotel just over here.'

'Fifty dollars is good for me,' I said, doing a quick calculation in my head. OK, so it was way more expensive that Miss Frances', but then I thought it would be all right for a couple of days.

'Also you need interpreter?' asked Cheng.

'Yes, I think I do,' I replied.

As we walked I explained what I was doing in Shenzhen, leaving out the precise details about the otter. When I'd finished he suggested that he might be able to set up a meeting with the Super Lucky Plastic Company Limited.

'Do you think this will be a problem?' I asked.

Cheng shrugged, 'Maybe . . . maybe not, I try tonight to sort it out, but it will cost some money.'

'Oh . . . how much?' I asked.

He stopped; a thoughtful look tiptoed over his face as

88

he sucked in his cheeks. 'Fifty US dollars for one day. For that I arrange meeting and my cousin take us to factory in his taxi and I will translate, OK?'

I dithered; was that a good deal? I had no idea. I mean, he was probably ripping me off, but what could I do?

'Yeah, that's fine,' I said. I suppose it's one of the things about being abroad, because everything's new and you don't understand the rules you feel like you're being ripped off all the time. It's not a good feeling, but I guess you just have to get over it.

We walked for another five minutes in the shadow of the soaring skyscrapers of central Shenzhen. The streets were busy, Chinese and Western business people walked purposefully here and there, blahing into mobile phones. I was surprised to see that the shops were almost exactly the same as those in Hong Kong, all the major Western chains were there. It was wasn't at all what I expected.

Cheng stopped outside this smart tower block with a porter in a blue uniform standing outside. 'This is your hotel,' he said, pointing to the main entrance.

'What? You sure?'

'Yes, very good price, not like Hong Kong,' he said smiling.

Before Cheng left I thanked him and we agreed that he would try and make contact with the Super Lucky Plastic Company Limited. We arranged to meet outside my hotel at 1.00 p.m. the following day, with the proviso that he would call me at the hotel if anything came up before then. After we exchanged goodbyes I stood and watched him for a minute as he trotted off back in the direction of the train station, then I picked up my ruck-sack and headed up the marble steps into the hotel.

The hotel was smart, all dark wood and brass fittings. I checked in and took the lift up to my room on the twentieth floor. It was huge compared to the Blue Lotus, plus it had an amazing view.

As I looked out over the city, I remembered the stuff I read about Shenzhen being not much more than a village twenty years ago. It totally beggared belief. I couldn't help but be impressed by the toweringness of the buildings and the marbleosity of the pavements and the sheer scale and complexity of the whole place. Don't get me wrong, in many ways Shenzhen is pretty inhuman, a hideous wasteland of tower blocks, motorways and concrete, like a lot of other big cities in the world, but just thinking about the effort and planning and human endeavour required to build such a place in so short a time totally blew me away.

Whatever.

As I looked over the sprawling city, I suddenly felt a long way from home.

*

I'd been working at Mrs Pretzel's for about a week and a half when my curiosity got the better of me and I decided to have a poke around her house. That afternoon I waited until she'd headed off down the shops and the bank and took my chance.

The house was surprisingly clean and tidy, compared with the garden. Unfortunately, most of the rooms were locked. In the few that weren't the furniture was covered up with dust sheets in a similar fashion to the drawing room and there was nothing else of note other than a few brass ornaments and some faded pictures of country scenes.

After about half-an-hour of exploring I made it to the top of the house. There were three doors on the landing. The first two were locked, but when I tried the third one it swung open to reveal a set of narrow wooden stairs. When I reached the top of the stairs I peered into the gloom; it took a little while for my eyes to adjust, but when they did I realised that I was in the attic. The only light came from a small skylight at the back of the room.

The attic was crammed with a mad assortment of junk. Shaky piles of trunks and boxes reached up to the sloping eaves. I picked my way through the morass, towards the light.

When I got there I stood for a second and looked around. On top of the box in front of me sat a pair of old, white, leather ice skates. I picked them up. The blades were rusty, the leather dry and cracked. By the side of the box I spotted four wooden tennis rackets, clamped in presses. I undid one and swatted the racket around a bit. It was weird, really heavy and small. I put it back in its press and returned it to the side of the box. I looked round and found a pile of books behind me. I picked up the top one and as I did a photo fell to the ground. I bent down and picked it up. It was a picture of a good-looking woman in her early twenties. She had long, wavy hair and she was wearing this tight-bodied dress with a pleated, flared skirt which did a good job of showing off her A1 set of knockers. She was sitting on the bonnet of a sports car which was parked on a long gravel drive. All in all, she was pretty hot.

I opened the book to return the picture, only to find that

it was in fact a photo album. On the first page there was a picture which looked like it was taken at the same time. The foxy girl stood in the middle of a group of people. She was dressed in the same outfit, with her arm around this handsome guy, dressed in a military uniform, sporting a thin moustache on his top lip. Around them stood a group of other people who looked about the same age. Below the picture someone had written: '1948, Aubrey and I at Blandfords, with Randolph and the gang.'

I was about to flick to the next page when I realised, to my horror, that it was a picture of Mrs P and her dead husband Aubrey. The cute babe in the photos was Mrs Pretzel. I fancied Mrs Pretzel. I was like 'How disturbing is that?' As I stood there feeling heavily creeped out, I heard her voice drifting up the stairs.

'Felix . . .'

She was back. I closed the photo album and replaced it on the pile, then navigated my way back through the junk to the top of the stairs, where I stood and listened.

'Felix . . . where are you?'

For a minute I thought she was going to come looking for me, but I heard the sharp click of her footsteps on the kitchen tiles, as she made her way out into the garden. I took my chance and headed downstairs. Mrs P was sitting at the table on the patio, reading the paper.

'Oh, there you are,' she said crossly, 'where on earth have you been?'

'Sorry, I've been answering a call of nature.'

'Yes, very well,' said Mrs P hastily.

A little later, while I was taking a rest from wrestling with a particularly obstreperous wisteria, I looked over at Mrs P. She was dozing in her chair in the late afternoon sun, a little trickle of drool ran down her chin from the corner of her mouth. I tried to envisage her as the young girl in the photograph, but I had to stop and resume work. The whole thing was far too distressing.

*

After I'd chilled out in the hotel for a bit, I started feeling hungry so I decided to get out of the hotel room and see if I could find some food.

Outside, rain trickled from the pewter sky, the air was warm, thick and sticky. I'd only walked about a block when I spotted the unmistakable frontage of a well known, global fast-food chain. Normally, I don't eat there unless I've got a serious case of the munchies or something, because it turns you into a fat chudda like Kevin, but right at that moment, I was bang up for some of their mutant filth so I walked in. The girl behind the counter smiled as I approached. She was pretty cute. I smiled back.

'Hello, sir, can I help you?' she said in tentative English, stepping forward slightly. When I'd finished ordering she smiled again. Which was totally weird, because up until then I'd never seen a happy person working in one of their outlets before. But in Shenzhen, they were smiling and their uniforms were neat and the place was clean. It was like some weird alternative reality; one where they don't spit on the buns and whack off into the mayo.

Having savoured my delightfully tasty and nutritious meal, which was incidentally very competitively priced, and is apparently a favourite of many of the world's greatest sports stars, I headed back out onto the street. OK, I know it's pretty sad, eating turdburgers when I was in the country that invented the Chinese takeaway, but

I don't know, I just felt like I wanted some kind of comfort food or something.

I wandered aimlessly for some time, checking out the shops and the people. After a while I spotted a sign in English for an internet cafe. I decided to check my e-mail.

The internet cafe was pretty basic, packed with kids all studiously hunched over their machines, in contrast to their peers in Hong Kong, who kind of slouched and smoked and seemed a good deal more disenchanted with things in general. It was also a lot quieter than the one in Hong Kong; the only sounds were quiet plinky-plonky music on the radio and the soft pitter-patter of typing. I sat down and checked my e-mail.

There was only one mail in my inbox; from my little sister Louise.

> **(No subject)**
> Felix,
> I just got a mail from mum, she says
> you are not working and she can't get
> hold of you on the phone. If you **are**
> up to something, **I will** find out.
> Louise

I should explain about Louise. Until about six months ago we got on really well, in fact, I could pretty much do no wrong in her eyes being her big brother and everything. When we were younger she used to follow me about everywhere and she was always wanting to play with me and my mates. At the time it was a bit of a pain in the arse, but in retrospect I suppose it's pretty flattering. She thought I was a pretty cool guy.

Unfortunately, things have changed. Just after my exams finished she totally grassed me up to my mother because she found out through her network of squeeby friends that I had got drunk at this party and puked all over the bathroom. She e-mailed a detailed account of the whole incident to my mother with a photo of the actual crime scene, taken on someone's camera phone.

Of course, I denied the whole thing, but my mother is a motherfucker when it comes to cross-examination and she didn't buy my line about hearsay evidence and that it could have been anyone's puke and where were the DNA tests to prove it. In the end she was so relentless that I decided that the best course of action would be to make a full and frank confession, or at least one that I sort of turned round a bit, suggesting that Jim had put me up to it and bought the drink, that I was led astray and that I would definitely try and reduce my contact with Jim and start seeing Kevin and the other Computer Club boys a bit more and that, as Jim had been having some problems at home, it was probably best not to be too hard on him.

Now, for a smart lady she was pretty happy to swallow my line about Jim being a bad influence. Mind you, she still gave me this massive lecture about the evils of drink and then imposed a range of punitive sanctions on my activities. As I sat in my bedroom licking my wounds I fired up IM; I saw from my buddy list that my sister was online.

ME: WTF
HER: ROTFL
ME: WTF!!!!

95

HER:	ROTFLMAO
ME:	Why?
HER:	Why not?
ME:	Whad I do?
HER:	U got born
ME:	This doesn't have anything 2 do with teh pony?
HER:	☹
ME:	My bad, sorry, didn't mean 2 fuXor it
HER:	Tooooooo fukkennn 18
ME:	Look, I'll make up 4 it . . .

My sister had been lobbying for a pony since she was about one or something and she was this close, but I fucked it up for her because she broke the keyboard on my computer (which she wasn't allowed to play on, something that has been conveniently overlooked by certain parties) and I got a little pissed off so I did some back-room scheming and briefing against the whole pony idea, by way of revenge:

> **ME:** Mother, I fully support the idea of Louise having a pony and everything, but how is she going to look after it when she's away at Dad's for holidays and stuff?

> **ME:** You know Mother, I really like horses . . . apart from one thing; the smell. You know they really hum and like it gets everywhere, but

96

that's OK with me, because horses are
just so lovable and cute and we all
know that nothing good in this world
comes without some sort of sacrifice

ME: Mother,   is   it   true   that
horses have the biggest fleas of any
animal in the entire animal kingdom?

Like a dripping tap of negative spin, playing on my
mother's worst fears. I should be a Tory MP or like the
president of the United States or something.

Anyway, it would seem that my mother attributed at
least one of these ideas to the source when nixing the
pony scenario, and my sister, who is nobody's fool, put
two and two together and the whole thing totally esca-
lated. It was like the Bay of Pigs, but on a way bigger
scale.

Since then my every move is being watched by her
network of squeeby, thirteen-year-old mates, who, in-
between getting fingered in the bogs down the park by
the local neds, and flashing their freshly minted tits to
filthy old perverts on the internet for Amazon goodies,
seem to do nothing else but spy on me and send texts
and picture messages to my sister. It's the total flip side
to the communications revolution, I mean, fuck Big
Brother; little sister is much worse.

I decided not to reply to Louise's e-mail. I wanted some
time to think about what I should do and I didn't want
to give her anything to work on; she was obviously still
harbouring a serious grudge. I mean, all of that was

months ago, and you'd have thought she'd have forgotten it by now.

Whatever.

When I'd finished using my mail, I paid the kid at the door and wandered back in the direction of my hotel. I was trying to work out the quickest way back when I noticed that I was standing in front of an Irish pub. A fucking Oirish pub in China. I had no idea the blight had spread that far.

I hate Irish pubs. I mean, I've never been to Ireland, but if all the pubs are the same as the ones in the High Street back home, then I tell you I'm in no hurry. Why would anyone want to drink in a place with broom heads and potato sacks nailed to the wall where the bar staff insist on dribbling embarrassing designs on the head of your pint? If all the pubs in Ireland are like that then it's no wonder so many Irish people leave the country.

The bar was sparsely populated (yeah, I know, but there weren't exactly many other options), with a few miserable middle-aged Westerners supping pints and watching what appeared to be some sort of formation aerobics programme on the big screen on the back wall. It was an odd scene. A small group of pasty, morose individuals, watching a large blurry image of this other group of lightly toasted, grinning individuals going for the burn on the other side of the world.

I ordered a pint of Guinness and took a seat at the bar trying to look and sound as nonchalant as possible. I relaxed as the barman started to pour the pint. He was Chinese and didn't seem at all concerned about my possibly being underage. That's if I was underage; I mean, what is the drinking age in China?

The Guinness was excellent, nice and creamy, with a proper head. As I sat there I found it hard to believe that I was in China drinking a Guinness. I suppose that marks me out as naive, right? I suppose if you're used to jetting around the world then it's not exactly amazing, but to me then, I couldn't believe it.

I was halfway down my second pint when a couple of youngish guys walked in and sat down on the barstools next to me. They looked to be somewhere in their late twenties, one a good bit over six foot, slim with thinning, blond hair combed back over his nut in a greasy slick, the other shorter, darker and fatter, with a little goatee beard and spiky hair. They were both wearing Manchester United tops.

'Awright mate,' said the shorter one in a broad London accent, after ordering two pints of Guinness, 'you in for the game?'

'Game?'

'Man U,' he said forcefully, like I was some sort of dullard.

'Oh . . .'

'You're not Arsenal are you?' he asked, interrupting me before I could get any further.

I was like, 'Fucking great: football fans.' 'No, I'm not really that interested in football,' I said, cool as a motherfucking cucumber. They both turned and looked at me as if I'd just nailed the ninety-five theses to the door of the castle church in Wittenberg.

'Definitely Arsenal,' said the tall one dryly in neutral, middle-class tones, before sparking up a Marlboro Light and taking a long, deliberate drag. The shorter one laughed. The barman handed them their drinks.

'You in Shenzhen long?' asked the short one.

'A couple of days. I've just come from Hong Kong.'

'Right. You here to party?'

'I guess,' I said, not wishing to contradict him again. The tall guy lit a second cigarette from the butt of the first one, I noticed that his nicotine stained fore and middle fingers were the same roast duck colour as the formation aerobicists.

'Well in that case you just got lucky, because you just met Shenzhen's two biggest party animals,' said the shorter one. Which should have set the alarm bells ringing, I mean, anyone who describes themselves as a party animal should definitely be avoided like the plague, but by that time I was on my second pint and feeling that there was much that was right with the world and that, as I was a large hearted and magnanimous kind of person, it was wrong to be too judgmental. Plus, I was glad to be shooting the shit with someone in English, even if it was about football.

'So you guys live here?' I asked.

'Yep, three years,' replied the shorter one.

'What do you do?'

'Party.'

'No, but I mean . . . seriously.'

'Seriously mate, we party seriously. We organise parties,' he replied, smirking over his pint.

'Oh, like what?' I asked.

'Anything from raves to corporate bashes; we've got our own company, our own PA, lighting rig . . .'

'Wow, cool,' I replied inanely, 'how's it doing?'

'Yeah, good, this place is a fucking gold mine, forget Hong Kong mate, this is where all the action is these days,' he said looking at his watch.

'Shit, Stefan, it's about to start. Oi, mate . . .' he said waving at the barman. The barman walked over. 'Go and do us a favour mate and switch on the football.' The barman looked a little perplexed. 'Football . . . television . . . you turn over,' he said slowly, pointing at the screen.

The barman smiled and picked up a remote control from under the counter and switched channels, banishing the team aerobics to the ether.

'Well done, mate,' said the short guy patronisingly, before turning to his friend, 'c'mon let's get a better seat.'

They both got up and were about to walk to the other side of the bar when the shorter one turned to me. 'You want to join us?'

'Err, yeah . . . I suppose,' I replied.

'I'm Gary and that's Stefan,' said the short one as we walked over to a table. Stefan turned and nodded almost imperceptibly, before lighting another cigarette.

The game was . . . well it was a game of football. Fucking dull in other words. I mean, I can't believe that people subject themselves to that shit week-in, week-out and, what's more, pay through the hooter for the privilege. OK, so I know it's cool to support a team now and pretend that you're the world's biggest fan, and that you've been supporting them since you were in the womb and everything, particularly if you're middle class or you want to be prime minister or whatever. But fuck dat shit; most games are totally boring. The players are all over-paid, drug-addled rapists and half the matches are fixed anyway. Plus, I found out about halfway through that the game we were watching was some exhibition match/marketing exercise. It was just a bunch of reserve players thrashing some rubbish team from Malaysia. I contented myself throughout the whole thing by drinking quite heavily, and by the time the game was finished I was more than a little caned.

After the final whistle, Gary and Stefan awoke from their catatonic state, or at least Gary did, launching into a seemingly never-ending analysis of the game. Stefan just sat there smoking like a beagle, occasionally nodding his head slightly or raising an eyebrow whenever Gary made some noteworthy point.

Just as I was about to sack it and head back to my hotel, Gary concluded his analysis and turned to me. 'So, Felix, what you up to now?'

'Dunno, I was thinking of heading back to my hotel.'

'Fuck that, come with us, we're off clubbin'.'

I hesitated.

'C'mon geez, it's just round the corner, we'll get you in for free. We do the odd night there so we know the door staff,' he continued. I thought about it. It wasn't as if I had anything else to do. I'd arranged to meet Cheng the next day, but that was at 1.00 p.m., so there was no big problem about getting up.

'OK,' I said, before knocking back the remainder of my pint.

Now if I tell you that the nitespot we went to was called Sexy Dreams II, you can probably guess that it was not exactly on the cutting edge of contemporary club culture. The walls were covered in crushed red velvet, the furniture was all chrome tubes and PVC; there was

102

quite a lot of neon and ultraviolet lighting smattered around. None of which seemed to deter the punters, because it was totally rammed.

The dance floor was packed with Western and Chinese businessmen dancing awkwardly with all these cute young Chinese girls to a punishingly loud karaoke version of 'Hotel California' by the Eagles sung by a young, highly made-up Chinese woman who stood on a small stage at the end of the bar.

Stefan ordered three beers and three whisky and Cokes. As we stood at the bar waiting for the drinks to arrive this totally hot Chinese girl wearing a really tight pair of jeans and a black crop top smiled at me and Gary. As the barman handed over the beers a group of Western businessmen got up and left one of the booths along the side of the dance floor. Gary scuttled off and secured it for us. I helped Stefan with the drinks.

A couple of minutes after we sat down the hot girl from the bar came up and whispered something to Stefan; he raised an eyebrow and stubbed out his cigarette, then said something to her in Chinese, not even really turning to face her. She frowned and then turned and walked back to the bar.

'Nice-looking girl, I think Stefan was in there,' I said to Gary.

He laughed. 'So could you be mate.' I looked at him quizzically. 'They're brasses, mate. Sixty dollars for one night in heaven,' he continued, a slimy smile spreading slowly over his face like a time-lapse film of mould growing on a bowl of fruit.

'Urm, do you . . . I mean . . . have you?'

'All the fuckin' time mate . . .' said Gary proudly, like

103

he was telling me about his new fitness regime or something. Anyway, as I didn't know what to say, Gary continued, launching into a rambling set of anecdotes about his sexual exploits in South-East Asia. I'll spare you the details.

As Gary chuffed on I drank my beer and looked over at the girl in the black crop top and tight jeans. She was dancing in a kind of exaggeratedly sexy manner with two drunk Chinese businessmen who were shuffling along gracelessly beside her at the edge of the dance floor. Gary spotted me looking over at her and said, 'Don't worry about it Felix, I was the same when I came out here. It was ages before I went with a brass.'

'What made you come out here?' I asked, hastily changing the topic of conversation.

'Well, I was with my girlfriend, and like it was all sorted we was going to get married, bought a house, the fucking works. Then I wakes up one morning, about two months before the wedding and thought, "Fuck this, there's more to life than being a fucking carpet fitter and marrying the bird you started going out wiv when you was fourteen."' He paused and took a sip of his beer. 'A week later I just done a bunk. Wrote a note, took the money we'd saved for the honeymoon and fucked off on the first plane to Thailand. Never been back to the UK since.'

'What happened to your girlfriend?' I asked.

'She freaked. Fair play to her and all. I know it was a bit rough, but she done not too bad out of it. We'd bought the house, and she got that,' he said before downing his whisky. 'She still hates me, but fuck it, she would have hated me more in ten years' time when she caught me porking her best mate or something cos I was so fucking bored.'

A drunk English businessman was now mutilating the corpse of 'Green, Green Grass of Home' on the stage to the drunken cheers of his friends. Stefan got up to buy another round.

'I'll get it,' I said, standing up.

Gary waved me down. 'Don't worry mate, keep your money in your pocket. We're making a mint out here.'

I sat down. 'How do you know each other?' I asked Gary, as Stefan made his way to the bar.

'Man U,' said Gary, grabbing the badge on his shirt and kissing it. 'Yeah, met him in that Mick pub about a year an' half ago, ended up in business with him. He's a good bloke.'

'He doesn't say much.'

Gary laughed. 'Yeah, that's true, fucking clever though, got a PhD innit.'

'How'd he end up here?' I asked, somewhat surprised.

'Same reason as me, wanted to see a bit of the world, and because there's fuck all for him back home.'

'You never think about going back?'

'Me? No chance, mate,' he said vehemently, 'why do I want to go back to that shithole?' I nodded drunkenly. Like, some of the stuff he was telling me was pretty hard-core and half of me was totally grossed out by it, but then the other half of me was thinking about how this would make a great story to tell the boys back home. It was the kind of thing that Rob, in particular, would have totally lapped up. Plus, by that point I was pissed, and when I say pissed, I mean proper pissed.

'I'm never going back,' said Gary. 'The way I see it, you've got one shot at life, this is not a fucking rehearsal or anything; so you might as well fucking enjoy it. What you got to do in this life is maximise the pleasure, minimise the pain.'

As he finished his little speech, a balding Chinese guy and these two really pretty girls sat down opposite us on the bench Stefan had vacated.

'Gary, my friend, how are you?' said the guy in pretty scratchy English.

'Hey Sandy,' said Gary, as they exchanged high fives over the table, 'may I enquire who your lady friends are?'

'This is Ji and Nu,' said Sandy grinning widely.

'Well Ji and Nu, this is my new friend Felix and I'm betting a pound to a penny that he's a virgin, so one of you girls could be in luck tonight.' I was like, 'What. The. Fuck?' For a start it was totally untrue and even if I was still a virgin there was no call to go saying I was to the whole fucking world. Fortunately, none of their English was up to much and they just sat there smiling, clearly not getting it.

'Hey Gary, man . . . that's totally not true,' I protested.

'Sorry, sorry Felix,' said Gary grinning, 'now don't go getting the 'ump mate, I was just fucking around. Look, what say you and I splash a bit of cash tonight and buy us a piece of pussy,' he said in placatory tones. I picked up my whisky and turned it round in my hand.

'You very handsome man,' said Ji, leaning over the table and touching me on the arm. I must have blushed so hard that even in the dim light round the table it was visible, because Nu broke into a fit of giggles.

'Sorry Gary,' I said ignoring her, 'but I've got a girl-friend.'

Sandy obviously understood what I said, because he turned to Ji and they exchanged a few words and Sandy pointed at me a couple of times. He turned back to me. 'Ji say that is a pity, you are very cute.'

Gary laughed. 'See Felix she likes you.'

I drank the whisky in one gulp.

'What's your bird's name?' asked Gary.

'Urrr . . . Julie.' Like, I wish.

'Nice?'

'Yeah . . . she's alright.'

'And she's back in the UK, right?'

'Yeah . . .'

'Well, Felix, my man, that's a long way away. We could get these two for the night and have a little party back at mine. What goes on, stays on . . . right?'

I started to feel a little sick. Stefan reappeared with a tray full of drinks.

'Budge up Felix, let the man in,' said Gary.

'Hold on . . . wait a sec, I'm just off to the bog,' I replied, getting up slightly unsteadily, realising as I did just how totally mullered I was. As I squidged out of the booth Ji leaned over the table and squeezed my arse, and everyone cracked up. I stumbled off towards the toilets, not looking back.

The toilets were through a door down by the stage. The drunken businessman had moved onto a mangled version of the 'Macarena'. Some of his mates were down the front of the stage, arms round each other's shoulders doing some sort of lumbering can-can.

I opened the door of the cubicle to find a fat whorl of orange turd sitting meditatively on the cracked yellow porcelain of the Asian-style squat toilet. I felt sick.

It took me ages to piss, like I had to struggle quite

hard with my aim to avoid disturbing the big dump, plus, I was completely hammered. When I finished, I opened the door and stepped out into the corridor, and almost walked straight into the back of this big Chinese dude. He turned and glowered at me, I stepped back and raised my hands apologetically, and as I did I saw that he had the hot girl with the black crop top and tight jeans by the throat; blood ran down her cheek from a cut over her eye, which was so swollen it was almost closed shut. The guy looked at me and then nodded with his head towards the exit, indicating that I should leave. He pressed in against the wall a little as I squeezed past him; as I did, I couldn't help but look straight at the girl. I have never seen anyone look so frightened. I pushed open the door back into the club, the dying strains of the 'Macarena' rushed into the small space. I didn't look back. I crossed the edge of the dance floor, walked straight past the booth, up the stairs and out into the warm, dark night. Then I started running. Running like the motherfucking hounds of hell were on my tail.

I don't know how long I ran for, but when I stopped and looked up I found, to my surprise, that I was standing outside my hotel. I felt like I was about to yak, but I managed to hold it in until I got to my room where I spent half an hour hurling the contents of my stomach into the nice, clean, Western-style toilet in the bath-room.

*

After a week of Mrs Pretzel kicking my butt at Scrabble I got sick of it and decided it was time to take action. I got my own back with the aid of a thesaurus.

'Toper – on a double word score makes fourteen.'

Mrs P looked at me.

'Are you going to challenge?' I asked innocently. She shook her head. Two turns later I got another one in. 'Legless.'

She looked at me suspiciously. 'Well that wasn't a very clever move was it,' she said haughtily, 'wasting two s's and opening up the triple word score for me.' I beamed back at her. Like I gave a fuck.

Three words later it was 'drunk'. This time she gave me a hard stare. I ignored her. In the end she totally thrashed me again, but I didn't care, I'd made my point.

The next day, I'm pretty sure she adopted the same tactic. She laid down urchin, ingrate, loser, slave and pauper. She still won so I might be imagining things, but if it's true, it's pretty sad. Both of us sitting there insulting each other like motherfuckers on a Scrabble board.

Whatever.

After a couple of further heavy drubbings I decided that it was time to take the whole Scrabble thing seriously. I found a website about Scrabble tactics which also had this list of totally obscure small words. Pretty soon the games started to get a lot closer. She still beat me, but there was never very much in it. I also noticed that she stopped getting tucked into the sherry until after we'd finished playing.

*

You know sometimes if you chunder after getting totally borked, it means that you don't feel so bad the next morning? Well, this wasn't one of those times. I awoke at 4.00 a.m. with a tectonic pain in my head and a raging thirst. I got up, drank a ton of water, and went back to bed. I woke again around 8.00 and couldn't get back to sleep. As I lay there I thought about the girl with the black crop top; I couldn't help thinking that I should have done something. But what? Step in and challenge the guy to a duel? He was at least twice my size and he would have ripped my head off without even breaking into a sweat. And if I'd told Gary and that lot, they would have just laughed at me. I suppose I could have gone to the police, but I'm not sure they would have been interested even if I'd been able to explain what had happened.

I spent the rest of the morning holed up in bed, watching Chinese TV, which incidentally sucks. In fact, it's almost as bad as French TV. There were like about eight Chinese-language channels, which all seemed to be showing this fascinating programme containing lots of footage of people shaking hands and all sorts of mad shit. And I was just about to turn it off when I stumbled on an English-language channel showing the same programme, which turned out to be about China's accession to the World Trade Organisation in 2001. Following that incisive and stimulating documentary was a programme called *English Language Competition*, where they got all these super-keen students from around the country and made them crap on in English about all manner of dullness, including China's accession to the WTO. I mean, their English was very good, but it wasn't great television. Anyway, just as I was starting to lose the will to live, the phone on the bedside table rang. It was Cheng.

*   *   *

Cheng leaned against the wing of a taxi parked in the rank outside the hotel. He looked smarter than the day before, in fact he looked smarter than me. I was wearing a shirt, but I didn't have smart trousers or shoes, whereas he wore a light blue short-sleeved shirt and a pair of black trousers. I noticed that he had also polished his loafers.

We exchanged greetings and Cheng introduced me to his cousin who sat smoking in the taxi.

'OK, Felix, I have arranged for meeting at plastic factory, but there is a little problem with the time, but I sort this out now,' he said, pulling a mobile phone out of his shirt pocket.

After a short conversation he switched off the phone and returned it to the pocket in his shirt.

'You have a mobile phone,' I said, like totally patronisingly and regretting it immediately, but I was sort of surprised to be honest.

'Yes, many Chinese people have mobile phone, it is very good price, better than other . . . how do you say.'

'Landline?'

'Yes, landline,' he said, evidently storing the term in his memory banks for future use. He didn't seem to be annoyed about my comment.

I raked around in my rucksack, found my phone and switched it on. About thirty seconds later a text message announced its arrival with a shrill beep. I opened it. It was from the local mobile network, welcoming me in English.

'Man, I had no idea.'

'Yes, China very modern. We are growing most rapidly of all countries in the world.'

'Yeah, the whole WTO thing has made a big difference,' I said, nodding sagely.

Cheng's face lit up. 'Yes WTO very important for China.' And then he went on for a couple of minutes about how important the WTO was for China.

'Who were you talking to on the phone just now?' I asked after he had finished.

'Oh, very sorry, that was Super Lucky Plastic Company Limited on the phone before, they can have meeting at 3.00 p.m. this afternoon.'

The factory was a little way out of town, in this big industrial estate. The place was super-manicured and it looked like pretty much any industrial estate back home, except for the pagoda-style roofs.

A gardener in a blue boiler suit looked up from tending a small bed of flowers as we pulled into the car park in front of the glass-fronted reception of the Super Lucky Plastic Company Limited offices. Cheng and I got out of the car and walked up the marble pathway to the main door which was flanked by two large stone dragons. I started to feel a little nervous. I looked over at Cheng and then down at myself. I couldn't help thinking that we didn't look that convincing. I still had my jeans and hightops on, plus my hair made me look like I was some kind of aborted genetic experiment that had escaped from a secret government laboratory. I'd meant to get it sorted out but, what with the events of the night before and the hangover, I hadn't got round to it. I briefly considered wearing my 'I Love Hong Kong' baseball cap into the meeting, but sacked the idea pretty much as soon as I thought of it.

Inside, as Cheng spoke to the cute receptionist, it

112

suddenly occurred to me that I didn't have a clue what I was going to say. I hadn't really thought it through. Unfortunately, before I had time to think any further, a young man in an oversized suit appeared through the doors at the back of the room.

'We are very happy to welcome you to Super Lucky Plastic Company Limited, if you would like to come this way, we can meet the board,' he said.

A large, highly polished table dominated the board-room. Around it sat about ten middle-aged Chinese men in almost identical black suits. At its head sat a large, fat-faced man in an expensive blue three-piece suit. They all stood up as we entered. There were two empty chairs at the end of the table. The young man indicated that they were for Cheng and I.

After we had all taken our seats, there was an awkward pause which was broken by the fat man at the top of the table, who said something to Cheng in Chinese. Cheng looked at me nervously.

'This man is Mr Huai, he is Managing Director of Super Lucky Plastic Company Limited, he says you are very welcome to Shenzhen and he hopes you have enjoyed your stay in our great city.'

'Tell him the same back,' I said. Cheng looked at me perplexed. 'No, not exactly, but just say, like who I am and how pleased I am to be here in your great city and that he has found the time to talk to me, all that kind of stuff.' They exchanged more words.

'He says he would like to know the nature of your business,' said Cheng, turning to me. I don't mind saying it, but I was shitting my pants. I swallowed my fear, picked up the rucksack from by my feet, pulled out the

113

otter, and placed it carefully on the polished table.

A faint ripple of what may have been either disgust or recognition flickered over Mr Huai's face. He said something to Cheng, who translated it for me.

'He asked where did you get this thing?' But before I had time to answer he said something else to Cheng. Cheng's face dropped slightly as he turned to me.

'He says if you here for business, what company do you work for?'

'Tell him it is my own company, I do, er, product design and that we are looking for a supplier for a series of statues we have designed, and that we saw this one and thought that—'

'Don't waste your breath,' said Mr Huai in excellent English. He stood up and walked round the table towards me. 'Why are you here?'

'Oh,' I said, 'you speak English.'

He ignored me. 'I repeat, what are you doing here?'

'I'm here for business,' I said as convincingly as I could.

'You do not look like a businessman, nor do you speak like a businessman. Why do you want to know about this thing?' he said, eyeing the statuette.

'Because, well, it's like I said—'

'I think you are wasting my time, I am an important man here. I have many commitments. I do not have time to deal with such insignificant queries. Consider this meeting over.'

I didn't know what to say. 'But, I've travelled so far . . .'

He ignored me and barked something at Cheng in Chinese. I was about to say something else but Cheng turned to me and grabbed my arm.

'No Felix, we must go. Now.'

He pulled my sleeve and stood up. I followed his lead. When we were out of the door, Cheng's face dropped.

'Felix, don't stop, he is important man. I think we have offended him.' Cheng's cousin was still outside. We jumped in the car and pulled out of the parking lot.

'What did he say to you at the end?' I asked as we drove out of the industrial estate.

'He wanted to know where you got the statue from.'

'What did you say?'

'Nothing. I did not know . . . Felix, this thing, you did not tell me. He is an important man.'

'So he knew about the statue?'

Cheng shrugged. 'So where you go now?' he asked after we had driven a bit further.

'I don't know,' I replied vaguely. I hadn't really thought. I was too preoccupied with the meeting and how badly I'd handled it, how I'd travelled all that way and blown it because I hadn't stopped to think it through.

'Maybe, you can come to our house for a meal. It would be an honour,' said Cheng, turning round in his seat.

'Ur, um . . . yeah sure, yeah that sounds good.' The whole otter thing had gone pear-shaped, and it's not like I had any better offers.

We drove back into town before turning off onto a smaller side road. Then we drove away from town again, through a big development of tatty high-rise flats.

I awoke with a start, unsure of where I was. I looked out of the window of the car. We were driving slowly along this dirt track lined with low, tightly packed breeze-block and tin huts. A group of kids playing football in

115

the road in front of us stopped to let us through. A couple of small dogs yapped alongside the car. Groups of people sat smoking and drinking under plastic awnings. Big piles of rubbish abutted the backs of the huts. I started to realise that we were in a slum. OK, maybe not a slum, but it was very different from the centre of Shenzhen.

After a short while we stopped in front of one of the houses. It was like all the others, a square, breeze-block building just over head height, with a corrugated iron roof, sloping a little to the back.

Outside a couple of grubby little boys squatted opposite each other beating an empty plastic bottle with short bamboo sticks. A small pile of burning rubbish smouldered beside a tree next to the house. I smiled at the boys as I got out of the car. One of them totally freaked and went running into the house screaming.

'You stay there, I introduce you,' said Cheng, before disappearing into the hut.

I looked around. I mean, you see slums and shit on the telly, but you have no idea. Cheng reappeared after a couple of minutes followed by his family: his father, mother and grandmother. Cheng introduced me to them and even the little boy who had ran away from me came out, though he spent most of the time hiding behind Cheng's mother's legs. Cheng disappeared again and came back with a stack of small plastic chairs and a table, ushering us all to sit down. There was an awkward pause while they all sat there and stared at me like I was a monkey in a zoo. Then, just as the silence started to get embarrassing, the little boy snuck out from behind Cheng's mother's chair, reached over and touched me on the arm, before running back quickly to hide again. The whole family cracked up.

Cheng said, snorting with laughter, 'He think you not real, like on television.' I smiled. When the general hilarity had died down a bit Cheng's mother said something. Cheng explained, 'My mother says that it is a great honour for you to come here today.'

I felt embarrassed, like I was the British ambassador or something. Cheng's cousin appeared with a couple of big bottles of beer and some glasses. I noticed that a few people had started to gather around us. The kids giggled and jostled each other while the adults just stood and stared, evidently discussing me amongst themselves. For all the Westerners roaming around the centre of Shenzhen, it was pretty evident that they weren't frequent visitors to that particular hood.

'You like Chinese food?' asked Cheng, passing me a glass of beer.

The food was excellent. Lots of different plates of fried meat and vegetables, which everyone shared. After we finished, the plates were cleared away and Cheng's family asked me a bunch of questions about Britain and shit, with Cheng translating.

Some of them were easy, like:

'Have you met the Queen?' which came from his granny.

Some of them were hard, like:

'In your country, are there many poor people?' which came from Cheng's father.

'Urrr . . .' I paused, 'like yeah, I suppose, but . . .' I stopped, I was going to say not as poor as you, but then that seemed totally derogatory, 'yeah, maybe it's a different kind of poor.'

'How do you mean?' asked Cheng.

'I mean . . . I don't know, it's complicated . . . are there many poor people in your country?'

'There are many poor people here, but we are lucky, we have house and permit for work in city. My father has a good job in factory, my cousin has taxi and my sister also works in factories too,' replied Cheng.

'And you . . . what do you do?' I asked, feeling a little embarrassed that we'd spent the day together and I didn't know.

'I am studying to be engineer, I have one year left, but at the moment there is not enough money, so I am working to help my cousin with the taxi and I also do translating. Next year I go back and finish.'

I didn't know what to say; fortunately for me Cheng's father had another question. He asked if I liked China.

'Yes, Chinese people very friendly,' I said smiling and raising my glass. Cheng translated and everyone cheered and raised their glasses and there were toasts all round. When it had died down Cheng's cousin said something to Cheng, who translated.

'My cousin, he says, "China maybe not such a strong country now, but one day it will be strong again."' I could hear the pride in Cheng's voice.

'Yeah, but what about communism?' I asked vaguely.

Cheng paused, looking a little uncomfortable, and then said, 'The current system is the best, we have the best of communism and also best of capitalism, we have very good leaders and they make very good . . . decisions.'

I tried a couple more questions about politics, but he totally evaded answering them, despite the fact that we were with his family and talking in English. I let it drop.

'Do you like England?' I asked.

'Yes, very much,' said Cheng enthusiastically.

'Maybe one day you can come to England and meet my family,' I said.

'Not in this lifetime,' he said with a resigned shrug of his shoulders, 'maybe in next one.'

'What do you mean?'

'You are very lucky,' he said looking at me intently.

'How?' I asked.

He looked at me quizzically. 'I think you don't even know the most valuable thing that you have.' I racked my brain. My PC? My PlayStation? My bank card? 'No sorry . . .' I said.

'Your passport,' said Cheng. Which came as a bit of a surprise. 'Yes . . . for me I cannot travel to your country just like that, not for legally anyway, in your country you have many things, here, so we are getting stronger, but there are many people and China is still a weak country. I cannot just go to your country. Is not possible.' There was another silence; again I didn't really know what to say.

'Sorry, Felix, I did not mean . . . it is not your problem; this is a problem from governments, not people,' Cheng said smiling, before raising his beer and kicking off another round of toasts. Then his cousin asked me all these questions about David Beckham and Michael Owen. I did my best to answer and pretty much agreed with everything he said. After that they talked amongst themselves in Chinese. I was pretty glad, the language gap, even with Cheng translating, was tiring. Probably was for them too. I sipped my beer and listened to the weird buzzing of insects swirling around the tree beside the house. The world seemed all fuzzy and warm. I was a little drunk, not like the night before, just nicely relaxed. Above me the stars shone dimly over the corrugated iron roofs of the shanty town. Home seemed a long way away. I started to think about the statue again. I couldn't help thinking that it was pretty random that I was here, in a Chinese barrio, because of some weird statue of a man having sex with an otter.

My thoughts were interrupted by Cheng.

'What you do now Felix?' he asked. I shrugged. 'Do you want to meet this man again?'

'What, Mr Huai?'

'Yes.'

'But, I thought he didn't want to see me again.'

'Well, I have been thinking, maybe tomorrow you could try to meet him when not in work. Maybe it would be easier if there are no other people there, maybe he is in better mood.'

I sat up. 'But how?' I asked.

'I think maybe we could follow him from work . . . in my cousin's taxi.'

'Maybe we can go tonight,' I said enthusiastically.

Cheng looked at his watch. 'Maybe it is not best, I think it is too late. We can go tomorrow.'

'What time?'

Cheng shrugged again, 'You leave with me, I fix for you . . . but it will have some cost,' he added sheepishly.

The next day we arrived at the business park a little before five in the evening and I was settling down for a long wait when Cheng spotted Mr Huai leaving the building. A little later and we would have missed him. Anyway, he got into this big black Merc and drove off. We followed him at a distance. He drove into the centre of town. After about ten minutes we were stopped at a set of roadworks. Mr Huai was two cars ahead. Cheng and I slipped down in our seats as we waited to be ushered through. I looked out of the window, about ten yards away these two guys were butchering a pig, right by the side of the road under this makeshift shelter. One of the guys wore an army uniform, the other wore a grubby brown suit jacket, a pair of combat trousers and flip-flops.

'Cheng, what are those guys doing?'

'They are labouring gang, they work on the road.'

'No those guys,' I said, pointing in the direction of the two men standing over the body of the pig.

'They kill for other men to eat,' said Cheng shrugging. The pink skin of the pig looked disturbingly human. As I watched, one of the men started hacking at its head with a big machete. I had to look away.

After we left the roadworks, Mr Huai drove through the centre of town and back out towards the docks. High-rise offices and flats made way for long, low-rise warehouses and big fenced-off compounds full of yellow and red shipping containers stacked up like outsized children's building bricks. It started to get dark.

Mr Huai pulled into a rough, rubbish-strewn car park, outside a small breeze-block building with a faded awning along its length. As we drove past I saw Mr Huai step out of the car and walk over to the door of the building.

'What is this place?' I asked Cheng.

'It is a bar,' he replied uncertainly. It didn't look like the friendliest place. I looked at him. He looked back at me as if awaiting instruction. I wasn't sure what to do.

'I will go in and check,' he said abruptly, turning to his cousin and saying something in Chinese. His cousin turned the car slowly in the wide, empty street, coming to a halt a little way from the entrance to the car park. Cheng got out and walked towards the building. When he reached the door he paused for a second, looked back in our direction, then pushed it open and walked in. The door swung shut behind him. A blurry cloud of insects swarmed around a naked bulb over the door of the bar. Cheng's cousin and I sat in silence, watching the door. After what I guessed was about five minutes Cheng's cousin checked his watch. As he did my mobile suddenly went off, my heart bungeed up into my mouth. I scrabbled to find it and answered without thinking.

'Hi.'

'Felix, this is your mother speaking.'

I was like, 'Oh shit.' My brain went into total hyper-drive. 'Err . . . oh . . . hi mum.'

'Felix, I have spoken to Dora today and she says she still can't get you on the home phone. I hope there's not a problem?'

'No, no, I was out and about this afternoon . . .'

'Very well . . . anyway she phoned to say that Mrs Pretzel would like you to start work again in two days.'

'Uh . . . yes . . .' Cheng's cousin looked at me. I opened the door and got out of the car, keeping my head down and talking quietly into the phone, 'Is she sure? Is Vespasian OK?'

I stepped away from the car a little, carefully avoiding a small pile of desiccated dogshit just by my feet. As I did I heard a soft but insistent metallic click. I looked up; directly in front of the car was a Chinese guy dressed in a black suit and an oversized black leather jacket, pointing a handgun at me.

'Felix?' the thin, electronic sound of mother's voice was so distorted she sounded like she were trapped in a tin bucket at the bottom of a deep well. My arm froze. Two thoughts flashed into my head:

(a) should I tell my mum about the guy with the gun? and
(b) I'm going to die a virgin.

The man gestured with his gun. He just kind of waved it at me, but I totally got what he was trying to say.

'Felix, I hope you're not trying to get out of this . . .'

I turned the phone off, banishing the tinny buzz of my mother's harangue to another place on the other side of the world. What was I going to do? Tell her that I wasn't at home, but was in fact in the dock area of a Chinese city and a man was pointing a gun at my head? She was in America. What was she going to do? Call International fucking Rescue or something?

And, yes, I know that I denied that I was a virgin earlier on, but what was I going to say? I'm nearly seventeen and I really should have lost my cherry by now.

I have fingered a girl, though I have to say it was not exactly the most erotic experience. Her name was Kelly Livermore, and she'd been like fingered by every other motherfucker in the school before me, which sort of took a little of the gloss off the whole experience, as did the fact that she was totally drunk. Plus, before it was finished (I'm not exactly sure how the whole fingering thing pans out, but I presume it hadn't finished) she puked all over the bed. Which I think had more to do with the fact that she had just pounded half a bottle of Aftershock and smoked a couple of joints of superskunk, rather than my amazing technique having driven her into a wild and uncontrollable state of sexual ecstasy.

Whatever.

The man indicated with his gun that I should put my hands on my head. It hit me with a sickening clarity, this was real, this was happening to me, someone was pointing a gun at me. It wasn't the director's cut or some extra bonus material or something; this was the real fucking thing. The man then pointed the gun at Cheng's cousin, who got out of the car and held his hands up. The man pointed at the door of the bar with his gun. As we walked towards it, another man stepped out and held it open.

The bar was small and dimly lit. A beat up, fake wood counter ran along the far end of the room, a couple of skew-whiff optics of Johnnie Walker screwed into the back wall behind it.

Cheng sat on a chair against the wall to my right. On the other side of the room a young guy in a black vest slouched impassively with a machine gun across his lap. A young woman in a green vest and a short black skirt leaned against the bar. Cheng looked petrified. As I stood taking all of this in, a door at the back of the room opened and in walked Mr Huai. He smiled a big, toothy smile.

You know at the beginning of this journal, like on the first page, at the very beginning, after that shit about hurtling through the velvety dark or whatever, when I said I was here because of Vespasian's prolapse, well, that's true. Vespasian did have a prolapse and if Vespasian hadn't had a prolapse, I wouldn't have found the statue of the otter and if I hadn't found the otter, I wouldn't have travelled to Shenzhen and a man in a black suit wouldn't have been pointing a gun at my head . . . but, you see, the thing is that Vespasian wouldn't have had a prolapse if I hadn't spiked his food with laxatives.

It's pathetic I know, and I really didn't mean for it to get out of hand. When I found out what had happened I felt like a pretty low character, and what was it Mrs P claimed Aubrey said? Character determines fate.

'Felix, what an unexpected surprise, I did not think we would meet again. I thought you would have more respect for my wishes,' said Mr Huai.

I said nothing and looked at the bare concrete floor; I could just see the faint impression of the grain from the planks that had been used to smooth it down. The grain of trees from ancient Chinese forests, preserved for ever in this unlikely setting.

'Well, what do you think I should do?' he said slowly, walking round to the bar and pouring himself a glass of whisky. 'Yesterday you wasted my time and embarrassed me in front of my colleagues, and now I find you sneaking around my bar.'

I said nothing.

'Why are you here, Felix, why are you following me from my office?' he said, moving out from behind the bar and walking over in my direction. He stopped in front of me and stared. I hung my head. He stepped forward and grabbed my arm. For a second I thought he was going to give me a Chinese burn or something, but instead he just yarked my arm behind my back and twisted like fuck. It hurt like hell.

'I ask you again, Felix, what are you doing here?' he said, leaning over my shoulder, his foul orc breath licking round the side of my face.

'Owww,' I screamed, slumping to my knees in an attempt to ease the pressure, 'no, no . . . I just found this thing and wanted to know more, I . . . I didn't mean to cause any trouble.'

He let go of my arm, spun me round and then grabbed me by the throat and hoisted me towards his face; he was a little shorter than me but a fuck sight stronger. I started to choke, his hands crushing my windpipe.

'This is not a time for telling lies Felix, I ask you one more time—'

'It's true, it's true,' I gasped, struggling for breath. He let me go. I bent over coughing and spluttering, rubbing my neck. He reached into his jacket pocket and pulled out a gun.

'This gun, Felix, do you know what it is?' he asked, carefully turning it over in his hands, as if he were examining a piece of rare porcelain.

'Nnno,' I stammered.

'It's a Glock 9mm, it has a polymer frame, it's light and very reliable; it almost never misfires. It is a very good gun. Made in Austria to a very high standard of workmanship . . . not like Chinese shit,' he said, cracking up at his own joke. 'Anyway,' he continued, composing himself, 'since it was designed this type of gun has ended the lives of many men and women. Do you want your friend to join them?' He leaned over and rested the barrel of the gun against Cheng's temple. Cheng looked terrified.

'No, no, no . . . please, I don't know what to say . . . I'm just a schoolboy, it was a stupid idea, I just wanted to know what this statue is, why it was made . . . honestly, please don't hurt him, he didn't even know . . .' I felt tears well up inside me, but I held them back. I couldn't think of what to say apart from the truth and the truth sounded so stupid.

Mr Huai looked at me quizzically, then swung round and pointed the gun in my direction. 'Follow me,' he said, before walking to the back of the room and opening the door through which he had entered. I looked fearfully at Cheng. His eyes reflected back my fear, but I could gauge nothing else. What could I do?

As I walked towards the door I convinced myself that I was walking into some sort of torture chamber with a metal bed frame, buckets of water, bulldog clips and car batteries or whatever. But when I stepped into the room I found to my surprise that it was more like some chill-out room at a trance night. The room was bathed in a warm red light from a pair of lanterns suspended from the ceiling; calligraphic scrolls and paintings of Chinese landscapes covered the walls. At the end of the room a small bronze Buddha surrounded by the red stalks of spent incense sticks sat on a low wooden table.

He shut the door. 'Please sit down,' he said motioning towards a small stool by the table. I complied so quickly I must have broken the world sitting down record.

'What do you drink?'

'Err, beer . . .' I replied nervously.

'Beer?' he said dismissively, 'beer is no good for digestion, take whisky, I have Johnnie Walker. Red or Black?'

'I'll take Black, please.'

'A man after my own heart,' he said smiling, the tone of his voice less threatening. He poured the drinks, handed me the glass and sat down. 'Do you understand Chinese concept of face Felix?' he said, fixing me with a forceful stare.

'Nno,' I stammered awkwardly. My mind raced trying to work out what was going on. If he was going to torture me why was he feeding me whisky? Maybe it was drugged. Maybe he just wanted to drug me and then bum me . . . maybe . . .

'Face is the system we have which upholds honour. It is based on shame and hierarchy, for some it is the curse of our country,' he said with a wide grin.

I said nothing, he leaned forward, so close I could smell the whisky on his breath. He was definitely more than a little drunk. But was that a good or a bad thing?

'I'm a big man in this place, I cannot be seen to entertain the likes of you and that disgusting ornament. It would make me look small, and that cannot happen. A lot of people depend on me, and I cannot have them thinking I am weak. Do you understand?' He held his face in front of mine. 'I cannot lose face in front of a schoolboy with a haircut like a diseased monkey.'

Then he leaned back and started laughing again, like he had just told me about his plan to take over the world. I still had no idea what the fuck was going on, but I laughed too, out of relief as much as anything else.

'Tell me Felix, what do you think of Chinese politics?' he said, suddenly, stopping mid-laugh.

'Umm, well,' I stalled, thinking of what I could say.

'What do you think of "one country, two systems"?'

'I'm . . . well, I don't—'

'I tell you what I think,' he said interrupting me forcefully, 'it's true, yes it's true, but not the way the Party says it is. They say there's one country and two systems, communism and capitalism and both can live side by side.' I nodded and took a big gulp of the whisky. 'But that's bullshit. Yes there are two systems,' he said, pausing for dramatic effect, 'one for the rich and one for the poor.'

He put his glass of whisky down on the table emphatically.

'But then, Felix, that makes us no different than any other country does it? Same in UK, same in America, rich get power, keep power and the poor they try to take it away if they get smart enough, but the rich spend a lot of time keeping it away from them? Right?'

'Well . . . I suppose.'

'Don't think I'm not a communist. I'm an important member of the Shenzhen party, but I also have other . . . wider interests, which I must protect. You could say: one person, two systems,' he said slapping his chest and cracking up again. I got the feeling that there was something a little rehearsed about this, like I was not the first person he'd trotted this theory out to. He poured us both another glass of whisky. I took a sip and felt it start to dissolve the big chalky lump of fear in my chest.

'Come, you have more Johnnie Walker and smoke a cigarette, these are very good, better than American shit,'

129

he said, handing me a pack with Chinese writing on the front.

'Sorry, I don't smoke.'

'Ah . . . no worry . . . sensible boy,' he said sparking up. As he did, I dared a little look around; behind the table on the wall was a traditional Chinese picture of a river and some weird shaped mountain peaks in the background. Mr Huai caught my gaze and followed it.

'Ah, this picture is of Guilin in Guangxi province. Many people say it is the most beautiful place in the world, a paradise on earth. It is only a short distance from here, maybe less than six hours by train, yet I have never been. Maybe one day I will go. Maybe one day I will have time . . .' he sounded wistful '. . . but now I am a very busy man, many people rely on me for their livelihood.'

I remember thinking how fucked up all of this was, I had no idea what he was going to do or say next. One minute he was quite happily waving guns around, and the next he was talking about the Chinese countryside. Plus, I also got this vibe that he was sort of confiding in me, like I was James Bond and he was Goldfinger and he was trying to make out like there was this mutual respect thing between us that no one else could get. I half expected him to say 'You and I, we are very alike Felix.' Which of course I'd have to deny and then he'd get angry and then there'd be a short tussle and I'd be karate-chopped on the back of the neck by one of his goons, and then wake up a little later strapped to a table with a laser beam working its way towards my plums. But that didn't happen. Instead, he started crapping on about his father.

'When I was a young man, my father insisted I was to be an honourable son, he said I must respect my parents,

130

I must obey him . . . that I wouldn't leave home.' A small, white elastic band of spittle which spanned the corner of his lips contracted and expanded as he talked. 'But I didn't,' he said, 'I escaped and made my way to Hong Kong where I worked hard and built up several businesses. I did what I had to and then when it opened up back here in mainland China I started to invest, to develop opportunities, I joined the party, and when handover came I helped.'

It was weird. I felt like he was trying to impress me or something, though who knows why he was trying to show off to a schoolkid.

'If I had not disobeyed my father, I would not be where I am today, I would be a prisoner of fate.' He paused and rubbed his mouth with the back of his hand, wiping the spit from his lips. 'I would be living in a little hut looking after my parents' chickens, eating rice and vegetables. I would not be here with my pick of any woman and as much good whisky as I can drink.'

Then he raised his glass and threw back the remainder of his whisky.

'Felix,' he said, leaning towards me, 'in this life you have to take what you can, because if you don't . . . someone else will.'

It was late into the night when I stopped crying. Almost as soon as I made it into the room back at Miss Frances' and saw the *Power Rangers* cover sheet the tears started. It must have been delayed shock or something. After all, only a few hours before someone had pointed a gun at my head. It was the first time I'd cried since the day my father left home to move in with Jill.

131

It was on an anonymous, grey day in February that my father left us. I came home from school to find my mother sitting on the couch screwed up in a little ball, her whole body shaking with grief.

She wouldn't speak at first, but I put my arm round her, which was totally weird, because, it was like a role reversal thing. We sat like that for I don't know how long, until she calmed down enough to talk. I knew what she was going to say before she said it. Don't ask me how, but I did.

'Your father's left us,' she said. Then she started crying again. After she'd calmed down for the second time, she started talking. She told me about how their relationship hadn't been so good for a couple of years . . . how three months ago my father had met another woman . . . how that morning, after I left for school, he had told my mother . . . how she knew it wasn't good, but how she never thought he'd walk out . . . how she thought they'd work it out . . .

'Who is she?' I asked.

'I don't know, someone he met through work,' replied my mother stifling a sob.

'Who is she?' I said again, fury rising in my chest like a flock of winged monkeys.

'It doesn't matter,' said my mother, extracting a large, soggy, mascara-stained tissue from the sleeve of her pullover.

'But—'

'Felix, don't. It's not her fault.'

How could she say this? Of course it was her fault. She had stolen my father, all I could think of was what I was going to do to the motherfucker, how I was going to make her pay and how the winged monkeys would pick her up by the hair and . . . if she had walked into the room at that moment I swear I would have killed her.

My memories of the next few days are a bit hazy. My mother took a week off work and cried a lot. My father phoned a lot. My mother refused to speak to him. He tried to apologise to me on several occasions and assured me that it was nothing to do with me or my sister. I just sat and listened, saying little.

At the weekend my gran came down from up north and stayed for the next couple of weeks. I spent a lot of time playing *Quake* on the computer and listening to my mum's REM greatest hits album. It's funny, you'd think that when you're unhappy you'd want to listen to something uplifting, to make you feel better, but in my experience it's the dark shit you want to listen to. I hate that album now, but I couldn't get enough of it then. I just wanted to wallow in self-pity.

In some ways the worst bit was my sister. Louise was eight or maybe just nine when it happened. To begin with she just wouldn't believe that my father wasn't coming back. She refused to admit that he could just walk away from us.

What could I say? 'Wake up you moron, he's never coming back.' Not possible. She kept acting like he was away on a business trip or something and that he would be back at the end of the week.

It totally slayed me, I felt so sorry for her. It must hit you hard at that age; at least by the time you're thirteen you've sort of worked out that your parents are human and maybe they can't beat up everyone else's parents or whatever, but when you're eight they're still kind of gods in your world. Imagine waking up one morning and not only finding out that one of your gods has abandoned you, but that he's abandoned you for someone else, someone who's a sales rep for a greeting card company, someone who owns a fucking show poodle called Maxi.

After the first week, things changed. My mother, never one to indulge in self-pity, got up the next Monday morning and went to work as usual. She got us up, fed us breakfast, made our packed lunches and dropped us off at the school gates. Not once did she mention my father. He had walked out, so be it. It was his decision. She had her own life to lead.

That's my mother for you. That Monday morning was when she resolved to start her life again. She just moved on. It wasn't like that for me or my sister.

I suppose I've pretty much got over the whole thing now, but I guess it still hurts . . . sometimes.

Anyway, I don't know how I got diverted onto that shit, particularly as I haven't finished with what happened with Mr Huai in his bar in Shenzhen.

Mr Huai sat spouting more stuff about tradition and opportunity, power and status, and I was starting to lose the thread a bit when he suddenly leaned over the table towards me.

'I like you Felix.'

'Oh, er, thank you,' I replied warily.

'You are not very clever, but you have some balls . . . so I think I will help you,' he said cracking up. 'Yes Felix, we did make this thing you have. We made it for a Japanese company, but they cheated us . . . no, not cheated us, but they went back on our contract. At the time I was most angry, we had an agreement. This is one reason why this thing made me lose face in our meeting – it is my mistake,' he said scowling. I frowned to show my total disapproval of the Japanese company's disgraceful behaviour.

'Now as you are an annoying sort of character I think it might be fun for you to go and annoy them too,' he said, pulling a small Filofax from his jacket pocket. He tore out a blank sheet of paper and then flicked to the back and wrote something down, before handing it to me.

'These two men I had dealings with, the first, Mr Uko, was the project manager and the second, Mr Itabashi, I think was the freelance designer.' I looked at the paper, he had written out the addresses of both men. 'Now, it is time you left, I have some more important business to attend to,' he said, laughing a dirty laugh and winking at me. I stood up slightly unsteadily and walked to the door, my legs were numb from sitting on the little stool. Mr Huai stood up and followed me.

In the reception room Cheng and his cousin sat with anxious looks on their faces. Mr Huai pushed past me and circled round to the back of the bar. He said something to his henchmen in Chinese; a look of relief swept across Cheng's face. Mr Huai grabbed the woman in the black miniskirt. She squealed playfully and tried to wriggle free.

'Goodbye Felix, and good luck,' he said, still struggling with the girl.

As we drove out of the car park no one said anything. I sat in the back of the cab and tried to relax, my hands were shaking.

135

Cheng turned round in his seat. 'Are you OK Felix?' he asked.

I nodded, 'And you? Your cousin?'

Cheng exhaled and shook his head, 'This was very scaring Felix. I not want to have anything more to do with this man.'

'Don't worry Cheng, I think I have what I need.'

'You find out?' he repeated a little incredulously.

'Yes . . . I think so.'

'So what you do now?' he asked.

'Is there a train tonight?'

'Yes, it still only 9.30 p.m., I think it is no problem.'

So that was that. I returned to the hotel and checked out. The bastards made me pay for that night though, and I almost stayed, not wanting to waste the money, but then I thought about Mr Huai, and I just wanted to get out of Shenzhen. When Cheng and I reached the station it was almost 10.30 p.m. Cheng walked with me to the immigration gate.

'I don't know how to thank you,' I said, feeling genuinely bereft, 'I am very sorry for all the trouble I have caused . . .'

Cheng had perked up a bit. 'Not to worry Felix, it was fun,' he said smiling and shaking his head, 'you come back? Back to Shenzhen?' he asked.

I thought for a second, 'I don't know,' I replied, honestly.

'Not all men like Mr Huai in China. I think maybe there are bad men in your country too?'

'Yeah . . . for sure,' I said. I looked at the board; I needed to get through customs and immigration if I was going to make the last train. 'It was very nice to meet your family, thank them again for the meal last night,' I said. Cheng nodded. I walked to the gate and handed my passport to the man in the booth. After I walked through I turned to wave goodbye to Cheng, but he'd left the gate and was following a Western businessman across the concourse.

'Mister, mister.'

That night, back in Miss Frances', I must have stopped crying and drifted off to sleep, because I had this terrible dream. I dreamed about my 'A' Levels again, which would have been bad enough in itself, but get this: instead of being in the gym hall at school, I was sitting at a desk outside Mr Huai's bar, alone in a pool of light in the car park, insects swarming round me.

I turned over the paper, the question was written in Chinese. My heart sank.

'Felix . . .'

I looked up to find Mrs Pretzel standing over me pointing a gun at my head.

'Felix, how many points would you get for "murderer" on a triple word score?' she asked.

I tried to think. I couldn't remember how many points an M was worth. Was it two or three?

'Come on Felix, your time's running out.'

I couldn't work it out. A big, hairy moth smashed into my face, I brushed it away and looked up at Mrs Pretzel.

'Sorry, Felix, time's up . . .' she said smiling ruefully.

'No please . . .'

I saw her finger squeeze the trigger and . . . I woke up in a knot of sweaty sheets. I swear, it was the worst dream of my life.

*   *   *

Despite the trauma of Shenzhen and crying for half the night, when I woke the next morning I was surprised to find that I felt pretty good. I had a shower and afterwards Miss Frances made me some fried rice.

'Where you go next Felix?' she asked when I had finished.

'Tokyo.'

'You need ticket?' she asked, quick as a flash.

Which is how, at 2.00 p.m. that afternoon I found myself on a flight to Tokyo. OK, so I'm making it sound a bit easy and if I'm being honest when I woke up I was pretty much thinking about sacking the whole thing and heading home. What was there to say Mr Huai wasn't just pulling my chain? Plus, there was the whole cost angle to be considered; the return flight to Tokyo cost another 300 sheets. But for some reason I decided to trust Mr Huai, and in terms of the cost I thought I might as well get hung for a sheep as a lamb, plus I didn't really fancy heading home empty-handed and facing Jim's 'I told you so' attitude for the rest of the summer.

Whichever way you look at it, Japan is the coolest country on the planet. *Power Rangers*, Sony, manga, Hysteric Glamour, *Transformers*, Shigeru Miyamoto, Gundam, Beat Takeshi, DJ Krush, Haruki Murakami, Bape, Cornelius, Read or Die, *Akira*, Evisu, *Ultraman*, Sega, *Godzilla*, *Mechagodzilla*, Studio Ghibli . . . the list goes on. I mean, have you ever seen Japanese kids? If you're up in town, you should check them out. They're always decked out in a mashed-up range of shit, from vintage denim and Prada leather jackets to like original Jamie Reid T-shirts and Converse high-tops. And they all do it immaculately, with an awesome attention to detail. In some ways it's a little creepy when you realise just how much time they must have spent getting their look down, but still, you have to admire their dedication. Plus, Japanese girls are pretty hot.

Narita Airport is also pretty cool, not as cool as Chep Lap Kok, but it's up there . . . which is so totally a line I'm going to use when I get back home, just casually slip it in at the right moment, when there are girls around. Of course with these things you have to wait for the right moment or you look like an idiot. Which reminds me, I

141

have to buy some trainers, so when someone asks me where I got them I can say Tokyo.

Whatever.

After making my way through customs and immigration, I bought a Tokyo guidebook and caught the Narita Express into the city.

It was getting dark by the time the train pulled out. I peered out of the window into the gathering gloom. The houses that lined the track were all built in a quite traditional style, however, as we travelled further into the city these were replaced by large, anonymous modern blocks of flats.

The second cheapest hostel in the guidebook was in Shinjuku, so I got off there. Large signs illuminated the streets, which were packed with people. It reminded me a lot of Nathan Road in Hong Kong, though if anything, there were even more signs and even more people.

When I got to the hostel they still had a couple of cheap rooms left, though when I say cheap, it was thirty quid a night. I mean, I paid about the same for a four star in China and the rooms in the Shinjuku guest house were tiny, even smaller than Miss Frances' place in Hong Kong. Anyway, I took a room, had a shower and crawled into bed.

The next day I woke at 1.00 p.m. I'd slept for just under fourteen hours. After I had a shower I dug out the piece of paper Mr Huai gave me in Shenzhen. On it he had written two addresses:

```
Mr Shiro Uko
New Day Product Development
```

334, Sunny Place Akasaka
7-chome, Minato-ku,
Tokyo 107

And:

Mr Hiro Itabashi
5-2-1 Ginza, Cho-Ku
Tokyo 170-3464

With the aid of the guidebook I sussed out that from Shinjuku I could get the Marunouchi line straight to Ginza, so I decided to head there first.

The underground in Tokyo is clean, punctual and totally packed, though trying to figure out the payment system was a bit of a struggle. Being in a foreign country can be difficult sometimes, and the simplest things can take for ever, things that are a total breeze when you're back home. But I suppose half the fun of travelling is that everything is new and interesting, even the little stuff like banknotes, stamps and street signs. For example, I observed that Japanese drivers switch off their engines at red lights. It's just a stupid little detail, but for some bizarre reason I got a big kick out of noticing it.

Of course, sometimes the little stuff can be a total pain in the arse but, as I was feeling pretty happy about how things were going, I inclined towards the view that minor inconveniences, such as getting to grips with the subway system, were all part of the fun.

When I stepped out of the underground in Ginza it took me some time to find the address Mr Huai had given me, and when I did, I was surprised to find that it was a private residential address in this newish block of flats. I'm not sure why, but I'd been expecting it to be in an office building. I checked the address; it was definitely correct.

I slipped the piece of paper back into my pocket, took a deep breath and knocked on the door of the apartment. There was a short silence followed by the sound of footsteps and the click of a latch being drawn back. The door was opened by a middle-aged Japanese woman. She looked surprised.

'Er hello . . . I wonder if I could speak to Mr Hiro Itabashi?' I asked tentatively.

The woman frowned and said something in Japanese. And I was just about to say that I didn't understand Japanese when she closed the door in my face. I stood still, unsure what to do. Thirty seconds later, I heard the low murmur of voices from inside and was about to step closer so I could hear better, when the door opened again. This time a much younger woman stood in the doorway, she looked a little older than me, but not much. I reckoned she was eighteen, maybe twenty at the outside.

'Can I help you?' she asked in slow, deliberate English.

'Er . . . yes, well I hope so . . . I'm looking for Mr Hiro Itabashi.'

Her face fell, like cherry blossom fluttering to the ground at the end of spring. 'I am sorry . . . my father . . . Mr Itabashi . . . he is dead.' I was like, 'Right, that's fucking blown it.'

'Oh . . . I'm sorry, I didn't—'

'Can I ask why you wanted to speak to my father?' asked the girl, interrupting my halting attempts at an apology.

'Er, well I wanted to see him about a business matter. I was given his name by a mutual friend.' Which was one way of describing Mr Huai.

'Oh . . . and what was it you wanted to see my father about?'

'Well, it was about something; something that I think your father may have been connected with, a small statue which I think he may have designed. I've got it with me . . .' I said, slipping the rucksack off my back and holding it up so she could see.

She looked at me thoughtfully, like she was maybe composing a haiku or something. Then she opened the door fully. 'Please come in.'

I was about to step over the threshold, when she stopped me.

'No . . . you must remove your shoes and put these on,' she said, pointing to these little blue paper slippers, which were deeply wrong in a fashion sense, but I put them on. I mean, when in Rome and all that shit.

The young woman showed me into the living room of the flat. I sat down and looked around. The room had a pretty traditional feel. The floor was covered in woven mats, pen and ink drawings of trees and mountains hung on the walls. The furniture was all antique apart from a big plasma-screen TV sulking in the far corner, because none of the other furnishings would be its friend.

I looked over at the girl. She was wearing a nondescript pair of stonewashed jeans and a baggy grey sweatshirt. Her hair was scraped back into a ponytail, which lent her a serious, slightly studious air. In fact, for a Japanese person she seemed distinctly unfashionable. Plus, she wasn't really that pretty.

145

'I did not catch your name,' she said slowly.

'Yes, sorry,' I replied, apologising in that totally reflexive English way, 'Felix. My name's Felix.'

'Felix,' she repeated, stumbling ever so slightly on the 'l'.

'And your name?'

'Miko.' There was a pause while we both thought of what to say next. It was Miko who spoke first.

'You mentioned a statue . . .'

'Yes, I bought it in England. I think your father had something to do with it.'

'Can I see the statue?' she asked. I pulled the statue out of my rucksack and put it down on the table just as her mother stepped into the room carrying a tea tray.

I really should have learned my lesson in China. The statue does not seem to go down that well with most people. I looked up to see horror and disbelief smeared all over Mrs Itabashi's face. Miko on the other hand remained impassive. She reached forward and picked up the statue. Her mother barked at her as if Miko were a small child she'd caught trying to stick its finger into an electric socket. Miko looked at her, then put the statue back down on the table. Her mother scowled and said something else. Miko turned back to me.

'My mother, she would like you to leave,' she said, the same serious, rather blank expression on her face.

'But—'

'Please, it is my mother's wish.' Miko got up. 'Also, please remove the statue.'

I picked it up and stuffed it back into my rucksack, and then walked to the door. I was about to step outside when I realised that I was still wearing the stupid blue

146

slippers. I slipped them off and bent down to pull on my high-tops. Miko opened the door.

'I'm sorry . . . I didn't mean to upset . . .' I said as I stepped out into the walkway.

But she'd closed the door behind me. I shuffled over to a low wall which ran along the front of the block of flats and tied my laces. Then I sat for a while and considered my options. I thought about knocking on the door again, but dismissed it as a bad idea, only likely to make matters worse. In the end I decided to write my name, my mobile number and the address of my hostel on a piece of paper and shove it under the door.

As I headed back across the huge, pulsating, super-globular macro-city, I couldn't help thinking that there was something funny about the way her mother reacted when I whipped out the statue. I got the feeling that she knew what it was. I mean, if she knew nothing would her reaction have been so extreme? But then I thought that if some Japanese kid appeared on my mother's doorstep and produced that statue from his rucksack, there was every chance she'd react in the exact same way. Whatever; the feeling of optimism which I'd had since getting to Tokyo pretty much disappeared.

The bit of Shinjuku I was staying in is kinda seedy, a mad mix of noodle shops, run-down housing blocks and nondescript little bars. I wandered aimlessly for a while, swept along by the human tide which coursed through the narrow streets. Light rain started to fall, so I ducked into one of the bars and ordered a beer. A couple of men wearing identical dark suits drifted in; they looked totally mashed, ties loosened, collars open.

*

147

'Gnomon,' said Mrs Pretzel, laying the tiles down carefully on the board. I scrutinised the fleshy folds of her crumpled face for a clue.

'Are you thinking of a challenge Felix?' she asked, smiling. 'Gnomon'. It sounded like a made-up word.

'What's it supposed to be?'

'It's not *supposed* to be anything Felix, it *is* the pin at the centre of a sundial, the bit that casts the shadow.'

I looked at her again; she was pouring herself another sherry.

For over a month she'd been kicking my arse all over the park and just when I thought I had her she pulled this out of the hat. I added up the points – 'gnomon' on a double word score was eighteen points. It would put her five points in the lead. I had nothing apart from 'id' for three . . .

'Challenge.' She sat back and smiled. I picked up the battered dictionary that we used and looked it up. '"Gnomon: pillar, rod, pin, or plate of sundial showing time by its shadow on marked surface."'

Game Over.

She leaned forward and picked up the green velvet tile bag, looking smug as a motherfucker. I lifted the board and tipped the tiles into the bag which Mrs P held open for me. Unfortunately, as I did one piece escaped, bounced on the table and skittered off onto the patio. I could see from where I sat that it was the Z.

I bent down and I was about to pick it up when Vespasian appeared from nowhere and fucking ate the thing. Seriously, he just rolled out his little pink tongue and lapped it up. All in full view of Mrs P. But who do you think got it in the neck?

'Well Felix, that was clever.'

'I'm sorry, I—'

'What are you going to do about it?'

'What do you mean?'

'What are you going to do about the Z?'

'Oh, maybe we could write "Z" on a piece of paper and use that . . .'

'Oh, no Felix, that would never do, for a start one would be able to feel it in the bag and the Z is a high value piece, oh no, I fear you will have to follow Vespasian around until he lets Peter out of his prison.'

I was like, 'What the fuck are you talking about?' Then it dawned on me.

'Sorry, you mean look through . . .'

'Yes, yes, Felix,' said Mrs P hastily, 'that's exactly what I mean.'

Seriously, she expected me to follow the hound around and sift through his plops for the missing Z.

That evening I got straight on the internet. A quick search revealed that you could get ten spare pieces for free from the manufacturer, but that it would take over a month for them to be delivered. I told Mrs P the next day.

'Felix, I'm afraid that does not butter any parsnips. I am not waiting over a month for my Z. Either find one from somewhere else, or I will start docking you wages, fifty pence for every day the piece is missing.'

'But you can't—'

'Maybe I should speak to your mother about this.'

'No, no.'

*

Back in Shinjuku I finished my beer, got up and moved on. Suddenly the rain upped a gear, people rushed to shelter in shop doorways, scurrying along, holding newspapers over their heads. I ended up under the awning of a noodle bar. The menu in the window was in Japanese only, but the pictures of noodles looked good and I was pretty hungry so I decided to go for it. Mind you, I had some major problems ordering. None of the staff understood English and I briefly contemplated sacking it and heading off to find a burger, but I thought that was a bit lame, so I persevered and with a bit of miming and pointing I managed to score some chicken noodle soup. I looked a little ridiculous flapping my arms and pecking at the ground and shit, but they seemed to get my drift and, as the food was excellent, a little amusement for the locals seemed a small price to pay.

I sat on a stool by the window and watched the rain beat down outside. The steam from my noodles rose lazily into the air. Suddenly it was 2019 and I was Rick Deckard, Blade Runner, on the hunt for five rogue replicants . . . but I felt tired and depressed and couldn't be bothered sustaining the illusion. I just kept thinking how stupid I'd been to show Miko and her mum the statue so early on, how I should have tried to build some rapport, explained more, found out about Mr Itabashi. Still, I thought, there was one bright spot, I had another address to check. Maybe I'd have more luck tomorrow. I'd certainly be more careful.

By the time I'd finished eating, the rain had stopped. I paid and left the noodle bar, spinning back out into the current again, drifting for a while, until a little eddy of people washed me into this blues bar. Pictures of all these venerable blues dudes who I couldn't identify vied for space on the walls. It was full of drunken Japanese businessmen enjoying themselves, winding down from a hard day at the office, to a soundtrack of suffering and defeat from another time and another place. I felt tired, maudlin and about a million years old. The music fitted my mood perfectly.

I ordered a beer and then another, and another, and before I knew it I was totally hammered. The TV at the end of the bar was tuned to a dead channel; the screen a meaningless blizzard of interference, like my brain – all jet-lagged and wiped out. My synapses flickered and popped in an ocean of bad chemicals. I could feel my cortical node shutting down, all my ports were blocked. An off-worlder came up to me, he had a prosthetic arm, a good one, looked like Italian workmanship, but I could still tell. He offered me three scarts of lithium hydroxyl, but when I looked they were cheap generics out of the dark labs in the new Japanese province out in Mongolia. It's where all the cheap Japanese shit comes from after they pulled their manufacturing out of China. I mean, seven billion dollars seems pretty cheap for half a country, especially when it's the size of Western Europe, right? But what do I know? Anyway, I told him to shove his black market junk up his hole, which gave his Transset some problems. In the end I had to just tell him to go away.

'No want your capsules, unerrstand?'

He shrugged, then grabbed me and picked me up from my seat, pushing me out of the door of the bar, just as John Lee Hooker or whoever started yet another song about how he had been dumped on by yet another no good woman; you think he'd learn.

Whatever.

I stumbled out onto the street and puked down my legs, all over my fucking high-tops. Three days, two vomiting incidents in two different Asian countries. A new record? The world span gently round me. People stared as they walked past. I tried to remember the way back to my hostel, but I couldn't. A little ripple of panic skittered through my muddled head, but then I remembered I was in Tokyo, the safest big city in the world in which to be totalled. Or at least that's what it said in my guidebook.

The next day I woke late, with a hangover. As I lay in bed idly thinking about Ji and Nu from Sexy Dreams II in Shenzhen my mobile went off. I dropped my dick guiltily and answered it.

'Hello . . . is that Felix?'

'Yes,' I replied, relieved to find it wasn't my mother.

'It is Miko Itabashi here. If it is possible, I would like to meet with you,' she said slowly.

'Er, yeah . . . of course,' I replied, trying to keep my cool.

'I will meet you at your hostel in forty-five minutes.'

As I waited for Miko, I checked my e-mail on one of the terminals in the hostel reception area. I'd sent a mail to Jim just before I left Hong Kong, telling him about the whole Japan thing. He'd replied:

Re: Brainfreeze mp3zzz
Felix,
Japan! Respect. Met any cute girls
yet? When do you think you'll be back?
Your mother phoned yesterday looking

152

for you. She is on the warpath big
style. You are due to start work
tomorrow back at Mrs P's, and she is
convinced you're avoiding her. What
should I say if she phones again?
   Jim

Start work tomorrow. Shit. Did that mean that Vespasian
was getting better or had he shuffled off to the big kennel
in the sky? I tried to think how I could put Mrs Pretzel
off. I was still thinking about what to do when Miko
appeared in the doorway of the hostel.

'Hello,' I said, standing up awkwardly, banging my
knee on the desk in the process. I winced.

Miko looked concerned. 'Are you OK?'

'Yeah . . . yeah,' I said, rubbing my leg. It hurt like a
motherfucker, but I wasn't going to admit that to her.

Miko nodded. 'Do you want to get some coffee?' she
asked.

'Yeah, sure,' I replied, before leaning over and logging
out of my webmail. I followed her out onto the street,
limping slightly and trying to contain my annoyance with
the world at large about having twatted my knee.

In the coffee shop we ordered and took the drinks to
the table. A group of glamorous middle-aged women sat
at the table next to us sipping lattes and picking at
tumorous muffins as they inspected their morning's haul
of shopping. Soothing elevator jazz trundled languidly
around the room.

'So, Miko . . . can I ask why you've come? I thought
your mother was pretty pis . . . annoyed.'

Miko picked up her cup and blew gently over the top.

She looked up. 'Yes, my mother . . . she does not know I have come today,' she said slowly. Her slowness was annoying. 'Have you tasted green tea before?' she asked.

'No. It looks nice, do you prefer it to coffee?' I said, containing my impatience.

She smiled. 'Yes . . . coffee, it makes me nervous.' I smiled back. She was odd. Despite my frustration, there was something about her that I liked. 'Maybe you would like to try some tea,' she offered.

'No, no . . . I'm . . . you were saying about your mother.'

A small cloud flitted across Miko's face. 'Yes, my mother . . . she does not know I have come today, I think if she knew she would be very angry.'

'Because of the statue? Did she think that your father made it?'

'Is your father still alive?' asked Miko, completely ignoring my question.

'Er, yeah, yeah, he's still alive.'

'Are you close to him?'

'Er . . . well, I don't see him that much. My parents are divorced.'

'Oh, I am sorry to hear this . . . but you still see him sometimes?'

I paused. I mean, the last thing I wanted to do was to talk about my family. I wanted to know about her father, not talk about mine. But I humoured her. I could sense that if I rushed it she might just get up and walk away and that would be that. 'He works for a big company and travels a lot, so I don't really see him a great deal.'

'What does he do?'

'He works for a printing company.'

154

'And what does he do for this company?'

'Er . . . I'm not really sure, he's in sales or something.' Miko looked puzzled. 'He doesn't talk about that kind of stuff much,' I added by way of explanation, feeling sort of embarrassed, 'he's with another woman now and you know I'm pretty close to my mother and my sister . . .'

She nodded and took another sip of tea.

*

It was about two weeks after my dad walked out on us that me and Louise saw him again. He picked us up in the car and offered to take us to Maccy Ds. Which got him nil points from the British judges.

Whatever.

I didn't feel like contesting his decision, but as there was no way I wanted to be seen in the one in town, I made him take us to the drive-in one out by the motorway. Not that my sister minded, she was delighted to see him and spent the whole time crapping on about what she was doing at school and what was happening at her horse riding lessons, etc, etc, etc. I sat in the back of the car and did my best to ignore them both.

Anyway, after filling us full of junk food he took us to the park where he pushed my sister on the swings and shit. I just stood there scuffing the toes of my trainers on the rubber matting, hoping that nobody from school would see us. Then my sister wanted a go on the roundabout.

'You're a bit quiet Felix,' said my dad as he stepped back from the roundabout, having given it a big push. I nodded sullenly, but said nothing, I mean, what the fuck did he expect? He'd walked out on us two weeks

155

before. My sister whizzed past looking a little fearful. My father had pushed the roundabout a bit too fast for her liking.

'Hang on Lou-Lou,' shouted my dad. 'Look, Felix it must be hard, I know . . . but I think it's for the best,' he said, half turning towards me, still keeping an eye on my sister. In my experience, 'I think it's for the best' is one of those things people say when things are really shitty. The human capacity for self-deception never ceases to amaze me.

'Your mother and I . . . it had just run its course, no one was to blame . . .'

Which made me as mad as an ant under a magnifying glass. 'Bullshit,' I muttered loudly.

'What did you say?' said my father angrily, grabbing me by the shoulder.

'You heard,' I mumbled, still staring at the deck.

'Look Felix,' he said grabbing the other shoulder and turning me round to face him, 'a), I don't ever want to hear you swearing again; and b), life is not as clear cut as it may seem to you at this point.'

I hung my head and said nothing. He held me for a moment. Over his shoulder, I could see Louise grinning broadly, the roundabout having slowed to a speed she evidently found more comfortable.

'Look Felix, I'm sorry, I didn't mean for this to happen,' he said contritely, 'I know I left, but I didn't leave you guys, it's just me and your mother . . . we . . . we don't love each other any more . . . we both love you . . .'

He went on like this for god knows how long, stopping occasionally to give the roundabout a little shove while I stared at the ground.

Whatever.

My sister was sick in the car on the way back, not much, just a little retch down her front. And I know this is fucked up, but it felt like a small victory for me.

When I look back I was probably pretty unfair, my dad was trying his best. OK, so his best wasn't great, but then he couldn't have stayed with my mother. I see that now. Plus, I certainly never made the whole thing easier for him, but I was only thirteen and it's fucking difficult to deal with when you're that age, I mean, no one ever tells you anything about that kind of shit. Like, they're happy enough to crap on about eskers and oxbow lakes and whatever the fuck else at school, but they never teach you anything significant, like what life's about, how you should live, what to do when your parents get a divorce . . . anything that might be of any use.

*

'What did your father do?' I asked, as Miko sipped her tea.

'My father . . . he was an artist . . . a toy maker.'

'Cool, what kind of toys?'

'He is most famous for Sleeping Cat, do you know this toy?'

I racked my brain. 'No . . . no, I don't think I do,' I said, apologetically.

'I think it is more for younger children and is maybe not in Europe so much. Here.'

She dug about in her handbag and pulled out this small, intricate carving of a sleeping cat all curled up on itself, its face buried in its stomach, its tail hovering above its body in a querulous loop. It was totally amazing, so small, so detailed.

157

'Yes, this cat it was made for me,' she said, 'it is netsuke.' I was thinking like, 'What the fuck's that?', but Miko obviously sussed that I didn't know and explained. Apparently, netsuke are small carved toggles which were attached to cords and used to secure pouches to the belts of kimonos. The one Miko showed me was about the size of a hen's egg. As she talked, I turned the sleeping cat over in my hands; I couldn't get over how amazing the detail was, just like the otter.

'My father, he made this netsuke for me when I was a young girl,' she said, 'and I loved it so much I asked him to tell me some stories about the sleeping cat.' I handed her the netsuke, she took it and looked at it. 'Yes,' she said, a sad look drifting across her face, 'so then he made up some stories in which the sleeping cat would have adventures, but all the adventures were dreams and then at the end he would wake up, yawn and then go back to sleep. They always ended with the same sentence . . .' She paused, evidently trying to translate the line into English in her head.

'. . . "Sleeping Cat yawned, he was still a little tired, "Maybe," he thought, "it is time for a little sleep.""' She smiled after she finished, I smiled back. The whole sleeping cat thing was so totally Japanese, like all that Hello Kitty, Yoshi Mori, Sanrio cutesy kind of shit that my sister was right into until about last year.

'Then when I kept annoying my father for stories he drew me some Sleeping Cat cartoons to go with the netsuke. It was then that Sleeping Cat became not just my toy,' she said with a pained look.

'How?' I asked quietly.

158

'Well, my friend saw the carvings and the cartoons and she wanted a copy, so my dad carved her one and made a photocopy of the cartoon. Then soon after all of my friends wanted one . . .' She leaned over and pushed her cup along the table, lining it up neatly with my now empty coffee cup.

'The father of another friend worked for a publisher,' she said, still fiddling with the cup, 'he persuaded my father that they should start a company together; my father did the creative work while he looked after the business side.'

'It was a great success, suddenly my Sleeping Cat was everywhere; there was a cartoon on television; books in the shops and all the people at school had Sleeping Cat dolls and . . .' She started crying quietly. Tears trickled slowly down her cheeks. 'I miss my father,' she said staring out of the window, turning her head away from me. I didn't know how to respond. There was a long, jazz-filled silence. She wiped her eyes with a handkerchief before continuing.

'Yes, when he died, it was very difficult. He was under a lot of pressure.'

'Oh . . .'

'Yes, he was just a toy maker, he carved toys and drew cartoons and then Sleeping Cat was a huge success . . . it was very difficult for him.'

'How?'

'He was not a businessman, he didn't like that, but he was forced into this world of money and suddenly many people depended on him, company men put pressure on him with new projects, many different things. He just wanted to make netsuke.'

159

'So what happened?'

'In the end he had . . . how would you say . . . a nervous breakdown. It was the stress . . . then his partner started scheming against him. He managed to get all the rights for Sleeping Cat away from my father, who was not interested in rights, he did not know their value.'

'You must really hate the man who cheated your father,' I said feeling angry on her behalf.

'I would like to say no . . . but a little bit of me does. I know it is a waste of my energy, but I cannot help . . . my father would still . . .' She turned towards the window again.

'Can't you sue him or something?'

'No . . . I think it is not possible, besides, there are other things in this world more important than anger and money. Have you got the statue with you?' I pulled it out of my rucksack and placed it on the table. 'Do you mind if I pick it up?' she asked politely.

'No, go ahead.'

One of the glamorous middle-aged women looked over in our direction. When she saw the otter, a look of revulsion appeared on her face and she turned away.

'Did . . . do you think your father made this thing,' I asked.

She paused, and looked at me with her dark, tearful eyes. 'I would like to say no, but if I am being honest I have to say yes . . . yes, I believe he did, it is his style. That is why I am here.' I nodded. 'It is funny,' she continued, 'I look at this thing now and it is so clear that he made it, it's like looking at his signature.' She smiled for the first time that day. 'It is so disgusting . . . I cannot imagine why he did this, he was a very simple man.'

160

'So is that why your mother was so upset?'

'How do you mean?'

'Do you think that she could see that he had made this?' I asked tentatively. She shrugged. 'Is there any way we could find out for sure, any way we could prove it was your father that made it, maybe find out why?'

Miko looked pensive, her face streaked with the faint traces of her tears. 'My mother, she has some of my father's papers at the apartment, but I do not think that she would approve.'

'This is important,' I said hurriedly. Anger flared briefly in her eyes. Almost as soon as the words escaped my lips I knew I'd blown it.

'I know it is important, but not just for you Felix,' she said, even more slowly and deliberately than before, 'it is important to me and my mother as well. There are other people involved, for you this is just . . .'

'What?'

'Well . . . why are you here, how did you get this thing?'

I told her the whole story, though I glossed over some of the bits with Mr Huai for fear of scaring her.

When I finished she looked at me thoughtfully. 'This is how you are here Felix, not why . . . why are you here?' I thought for a moment.

'Well, I'm not sure, but there's something about this, a mystery that I need to solve, I need to see . . .'

'Are you sure?' she asked sharply, 'Is this not just an excuse to go flying off on a holiday at your parents' expense? Is this not just a little bit of fun because you were bored?'

'I'm sorry . . . I didn't mean—'

She held up her hand, 'I do not want to talk about this

161

any more, I need to think.' And with that she stood up and left. I briefly considered following her, but I knew that even if I had caught up with her it wouldn't have done any good. Why can't you think before you open your stupid mouth, I thought; why do you have to be such an arsehole?

On the subway back from Akasaka I felt pretty low. I'd easily found the other address Mr Huai had given me, but when I asked at reception they said they had never heard of a New Day Product Development company or a Mr Shiro Uko. I asked again, but the girl shrugged her shoulders. By the time I got back to the guest house in Shinjuku, I had pretty much come to the conclusion that I'd blown it. One dead end and one wasted opportunity. And that was the most frustrating aspect, because I was certain that the answer lay with Miko.

Back at the guest house I logged onto one of the terminals. I fired up IM with the intention of getting hold of Jim for an update on the whole Mrs P/Vespasian situation; unfortunately he was offline, and I was just about to log off when I saw that my sister had come online.

ME:	yo
HER:	huh
ME:	sorry about the pony
HER:	not good enufff
ME:	I'll make it up 2 u
HER:	fuk u
ME:	Honest, I'll try
HER:	Y no sightings for my frndz in last wk?

```
ME:    Flu
HER:   Why no ansr fone?
ME:    Lost voice
HER:   What are u up 2?
ME:    Nothing, feel real baddddd
HER:   WTF
ME:    What?
HER:   244.100.98.87
ME:    ?
HER:   Japan? WTF?
```

I bailed. You know this is a fucked-up world when your thirteen-year-old sister is running a look-up on your IP address. I briefly considered my options and then fired IM back up again.

```
ME:    sorry IM crash
HER:   Japan? WTF?
ME:    IP is spoof
HER:   What?
ME:    Proxy
HER:   I'll tell
ME:    what you gonna say. 'Mum,
       Felix's a 1337 hax0r'
HER:   Maybe
ME:    Like she'd understand
HER:   Look I know you're up 2
       sumthing, obviously not in
       Japan, but up 2 no
       good . . .
ME:    Got flu
HER:   Liarrrr
```

```
ME:      So  wrong,  I'm  ill  *cough*
         see
HER:     Funny . . . I'm stepping up
         surveillance
ME:      Love u 2
```

OK, I know I messed up the whole pony scenario, but it seemed a bit rich that she was still acting like she was some sort of motherfucking robot nemesis from the future.

Whatever.

I think I just about blagged it. She admitted that it was impossible for me to be in Japan. Still, she obviously had her squeeb network on Code Red. One plus point, however, was that I had found my excuse for not turning up to work the next day. I'll admit it wasn't a very sophisticated ruse, but what else could I do? I fired off an e-mail to my mother explaining that I'd been struck down by the lurgy and one to Jim, pleading with him to stand in for me, in the hope that this would help reduce the heat.

After I logged off, I went back up to my room and spent the afternoon writing up this diary. As I did I got more and more and more depressed. I felt like I was so close but yet so far. I'd sort of worked out that the statue was probably made by Miko's dad, but I still didn't really know why. I still didn't know what the statue was about or why he'd made it or what exactly the link was with Super Lucky Plastic Company Limited. I was just about to head downstairs to score some graze when my mobile went off.

'Felix, it is Miko Itabashi speaking.'

'Er, yeah, good to hear from you . . .' I replied, trying to suppress my excitement.

'I wanted to say that my mother has gone out for the

164

evening. If you would like to look through my father's papers, you must come around straight away.'

Forty-five minutes later I stood at her door in Ginza.

'Come in,' she said. I removed my high-tops, slipped on the blue paper pumps and followed her into the living room.

'These are my father's papers,' said Miko pointing to three piles which sat on the coffee table. 'I have sorted them into three groups: on the left are ones from the early part of his career, in the middle is from the time he worked in the big company, and the final pile, on the right, is from after the time he left the company. However, most papers are in Japanese, so I think you cannot be of much help.'

'Oh,' I replied, 'is there anything I can do?'

'I think there are some files in English, mainly to be concerned with rights deal with American and sometimes British publishers for the Sleeping Cat. They are on top of the middle pile.'

I zipped through the few English files pretty quickly and by the time I'd finished, Miko was still only about a third of the way down the left-hand pile. As I hadn't found anything I got up and wandered round the room. The small cabinet on the far wall was covered with family photos, including shots of a man I took to be her father. He had the same serious, sad face as her. I looked over and watched as she read. She had a long face and quite a flat nose, and whilst she wasn't what you'd call classically beautiful, there was something about her, she had an air of calm prepossession, which was quite appealing. Don't get me wrong, she was nice, but I didn't fancy her or anything.

Whatever.

I picked up a remote control which lay on the edge of the table and switched on the TV. Miko looked up at me with an annoyed expression on her face.

'Felix, if you must to watch television, please turn the noise down so I can think.' I turned the volume down and flicked through a bunch of channels. From what I could see Japanese TV sucks even harder than your mother. All I could find was either *Dragonball Z* stylee kiddie manga with animation rates of about one frame per hour or karaoke-type pop shows with tweenie jail-bait dressed in these totally harsh primary colours.

I eventually alighted on this channel with a stunning babe who was talking to an oldish geezer in a tweed jacket. I spent a little while trying to work out what was going on. I thought he might be some sort of writer, because she had a book in her hands which she would periodically hold up to the camera. I had no idea what she was saying, but she was doing a lot of hair tossing, which in my experience is a really bad sign.

'Er, sorry to interrupt and everything, but what is she saying?' I asked Miko.

Miko frowned, but put down the letter she was reading and stared at the TV with a look of intense concentration. 'She is trying to pretend that she has read his book. She is a model and TV presenter in this country and she is very famous. She does interviews like this to make her seem as if she is intelligent as well.'

'I could totally tell that. It was all that hair tossing she was doing,' I said enthusiastically, pretending to flick my hair with my hand.

Miko smiled. 'Yes, very good Felix, but I do not think you are one to be talking about other people's hair.'

I'd completely forgotten about my hair. It wasn't as bad as it had been a couple of days before, but it was still pretty fucked up, but what with all the stuff that had been going on, I'd had no time to do anything about it. I explained to Miko about the hairdressers in Hong Kong.

'Well, maybe I can help you,' she said when she'd stopped laughing

'How?'

'Maybe I can cut it so it looks a little better . . . but only if you switch off the television and start looking through these files. I think maybe there are some other English letters in the right-hand pile also.'

About half an hour later she suggested we take a break. She disappeared into the kitchen and came back with a couple of cans of Coke and a bag of rice crackers. I hadn't found any more in the English files.

'How are you out here?' she asked, as I opened one of the cans.

'What do you mean?'

'How do you afford this journey, it must be very expensive?' I explained about the emergency bank card and the university fund. 'But it seems stupid to waste all the money that has been put aside for your education, it seems very . . . frivolous,' she said, frowning. I looked down at the matting floor. 'When do you go to university?'

'At the end of this summer.'

'Oh, and what do you do when you get there?'

'Well, I'm signed up to study commercial law . . .' I replied, hesitantly.

'You do not sound very sure.'

I shrugged, 'I dunno, I guess I'll do law. I'm not really sure exactly what I want to do . . .' I said feeling a little embarrassed. 'What do you do?' I asked quickly.

'I am a trainee social worker. I work with disadvantaged children. It is always what I have wanted to do, I very much like working with people and now Japan has more and more social problems, so it is important.'

'Doesn't it get you down, having to deal with other people's problems every day?'

She nodded, 'Sometimes I wonder if I am doing any good, but then I think it is important to help others. If I get depressed about my work, I try to imagine what the world would be like if I didn't make an effort . . . if none of us made an effort for other people.' She looked at me intently, then smiled slightly. 'Anyway, it is what makes me happy. I think this is what you need to find . . . am I right, Felix?'

About half an hour later I found it, near the bottom of the right-hand pile.

'Here Miko – look, look, I think this might be something,' I said, jumping up and waving a small bundle of e-mails. There were four, the first was dated January 17, 1997:

RE: Otter Commission
```
I regret to say that I will not be
able to undertake the work you wish
to commission, I feel that there is
something in this work which I can
not do.
   Yours,
   Hiro Itabashi
```

I handed it to Miko; she read it carefully. 'He must have had this translated,' she mused, 'he could not speak or write English.'

There were three more mails in the bundle:

Increased Offer

Mr Banks understands that you are a busy man and may have some reservations about undertaking this commission; however, he is very keen that you do this; he has long admired your work and believes that your style is absolutely right for this piece. In this light he has offered to increase your fee from $25,000 to $50,000, and would also be prepared to sign a contract ensuring your complete anonymity. I have separately engaged a product manager who would oversee the production process in China. You would only be required to make one trip over to the country to sign off on the finished product. You would not be required to have any management responsibility for the actual production of the piece.

Yours sincerely,
Howard Tripp
Attorney-at-Law
1010 Ocean Heights Boulevard
San Francisco

RE: Increased Offer

Thank you for the copy of the proposed contract, I can confirm that in light of the increased offer and the new clauses I will now undertake the work. I would be grateful if your client could send me initial sketches and any other relevant material. I will have a preliminary model ready in two weeks' time. Please find enclosed my signed copy of the contract and my bank account details for payment of the first instalment. Again I have to repeat, complete confidentiality is most important in this case.

Hiro Itabashi

RE: Product Manager

The name of the product manager we have engaged is Mr Shiro Uko. He has extensive experience managing Chinese suppliers and has worked on several high profile product launches. Please feel free to contact him; he will help you with some of the logistical issues. In addition, Joe is keen to know if you will be in the US in the near future as he would like to meet you.

Howard Tripp
Attorney-at-Law
1010 Ocean Heights Boulevard
San Francisco

'The product manager – that's the other name Mr Huai gave me, that's the guy I tried to find this afternoon,' I said. I handed the e-mails to Miko. She sat reading them, while I bounced around the room.

'But who is this Mr Banks and who's Joe?' asked Miko when she'd finished.

I sat down and read the e-mails again. 'Do you think that Mr Banks is the same guy as Joe, in the last mail?' I asked.

Miko shrugged. 'The last date here is March 1997. This is after the time that my father lost his control of the company. This is shortly before he died,' she said, her sadness filling the small room like iron filings. 'I knew it was my father's work,' she continued slowly, 'but I still cannot to understand.'

I could see how this pained her. I felt like I had turned up and informed her that I was her father's secret love child or something. I could see how this might totally change her view of him. After all, there's a pretty big difference between Sleeping Cat and Bald Man Sodomising Otter.

'I'm sorry,' I said, 'I shouldn't have . . . maybe it would have been better if you didn't know.'

She looked at me and smiled a small, sad smile. 'No Felix, it is not your fault, it is the truth, and the truth often finds some way to make it out.' Then she laughed, leaned forward and touched my arm.

'What are you laughing at?' I asked, perplexed by her sudden change of mood.

'Your hair, Felix, really, we must do something.'

'But what about the rest of the papers?'

'They can wait. My mother will not be back for some time yet.'

*

171

Jill's quite a bit younger than my mother. Jim reckons she's quite cute, but I refuse to see her in that way.

The first time I met her was about two months after my father left us. He picked us up from the house to take us to this safari park. Anyway, Jill was in the front seat and I was in the back with Louise. In between us sat Maximillian, Liege of the Faerie Kings. Maxi, as he is more commonly known, is Jill's show-poodle. He's one of the big ones, but he still looks like a total numpty on account of his ludicrous hairdo. Jill spends ages with hairspray and a hairdryer primping his horrible little butt balls and whatever.

Anyway, Jill was sitting in the front seat, sort of half turned round to face us, trying to ingratiate her way into our affections, and Louise was totally falling for the whole thing and blahing away about how she wanted to get a pony. I on the other hand was maintaining a dignified silence and staring out of the window emitting the occasional grunt if Jill directed a question at me.

After a bit my dad asked Jill to read the map, so she turned round to face the front. As soon as she did Maxi spotted his chance. The disgusting beast squatted up on his haunches and whammed his front paws over my shoulders. I struggled valiantly, but he was a pretty big dog and I had my seat belt on. There was nothing I could do. He thrust his loin against my arm and started humping frantically. His head was right next to mine, his bright pink tongue lolling out of his mouth, his eyes crossed in delirious concentration. His hot, meaty breath wafted over me in foul gusts as he pumped away.

Jill leaned through the seats and tried to grab him, but he was too strong. In the end my dad had to stop the car on the hard shoulder and it took the combined efforts of both him and Jill to prise the repulsive hound off me.

For the rest of the journey Jill sat in the back with Maxi and Louise. When we got to the safari park I got out of the car. It was pretty hot so I grabbed the bottom of my hoody, intending to remove it. As I did, I put my hand in something warm and sticky. It was poodle spuzz.

*

As Miko cut my hair, I tried to work out what was going on in the e-mails I had found. It seemed that Miko's dad had been commissioned to design the statue, which had then been mass produced in China, so presumably there was more than one of them around. But who was Howard Tripp? And, more importantly, who was Joe Banks and why had he commissioned Miko's father to make the otter?

'Lift head up,' said Miko, slipping her hand gently under my chin. She resumed cutting and more hair fell onto the sheet of newspaper she had laid under the chair. When she leaned in close I could feel her soft breath on my neck.

'What do you do next?' she asked, standing in front of me squinting, with the scissors in her hand.

'Good question. I don't know . . . maybe I'll go to San Francisco,' I laughed nervously.

'OK, hair is finished,' she said, handing me a small mirror. And I have to say, given the mess she had to work with, I reckon she did an excellent job. I stood up and like, I don't know how it happened, but I just kind of spontaneously hugged her. Then I got embarrassed so I let go.

She stood there and smiled. 'You could just have said

thank you. But it is very nice Felix. I think we check rest of papers now, before my mother comes home.'

We spent two more hours searching through the remaining papers, but nothing further came to light. When we had finished Miko looked at her watch and said, 'I think it is time for you to go, my mother will be back home in one hour and she must not find you here.'

As I walked to the underground I felt a hot prickle of guilt run up my spine as I remembered how sad Miko had looked when she read the e-mails I found. I should have been happy, you know, I was back on the right track, but, like, I just felt I'd totally blundered into someone's life and fucked it up with no thought of the consequences. Miko had been pretty nice about it all, but I could see that it was painful for her. Before I left we exchanged e-mail addresses and I promised to keep in touch and tell her if I found out more. It seemed the least I could do.

The next day I had things to do and decisions to make. First off I checked my mail. There was one from my mother:

Having a Whale of a Time
Felix,
Sandra and I have made it to Maine! We spent the day whale-watching, which was fantastic. Sandra took some great pictures with the new digital camera I bought her. I'm sorry to hear that you're ill, however, I also hope that you are not using some minor ailment

as an excuse to malinger. If you are genuinely ill then I fully understand that you cannot work for Mrs Pretzel. I am pleased to hear that you have arranged for Jim to take over in your absence. This was a mature solution to the problem, but if I do find out that you are up to no good, I will come down on you like a ton of bricks.
Love,
Mum

I sent a mail to my mother reassuring her that I was definitely suffering, and one to Jim thanking him for standing in.

Then, I ran an internet search on Banks. About a million results rippled down the page. I opened the first one, which was an article from the *San Francisco Independent Times*:

An Artistic Temperament
Our Arts Correspondent, Dave Hitzker, got more than he bargained for when he managed to track down reclusive artist, Joseph Banks.

Joseph Banks, sixty, is one of this country's most intriguing artists. Over the last thirty years, he's produced a body of work that puts him up there with Andy, Jackson and the other greats of the American post-war art scene. However, just over five years ago, when seemingly still at the height of his powers, he suddenly quit the art world, severing his famously successful relationship with super-agent Howard Tripp and announcing his intention never to exhibit again.

Banks now lives as a virtual recluse in his beautiful northern California home near the small coastal town of Puerto Novo. Which is where I found myself on a sunny day in May earlier this year, following in the footsteps of the steady flow of devotees and acolytes from all around the world who come to meet the man *New Yorker* magazine called 'America's Greatest Living Artist'.

Puerto Novo is an idyllic spot, an old fishing village huddled in the shelter of a small bay in the otherwise rugged north California coast; it has long been a favorite retreat for artists and writers. Banks lives a couple of miles north of town, in a secluded log cabin. It was there that I headed first. It took me some time to locate the small dirt track which leads from the public highway to his property; having done so I followed it into the forest until I found the road blocked by a large, metal gate set in a high, chain-link fence topped with razor wire. I buzzed the intercom and waited. There was no reply. Undeterred, I drove back into town where I decided to do some asking around, to see what the people of Puerto Novo made of their most famous fellow resident. Many people were reluctant to talk; I did find one man, Mr Buddy Novak, a long-term resident of the town, who was willing to speak. He exclusively revealed to me that his nephew, Johnny, had done some work on Mr Banks's drains. I also discovered from Mr Novak that, in common with the rest of the population of Puerto Novo, Mr Banks probably shopped at the local mini-mall on the outskirts of town. It was there that I headed next.

This time my luck was in, as I hadn't been in the car park for much more than half an hour when who should pull up in a beat-up old Volvo, but Joseph Banks. Despite the fact that he hasn't been photographed in almost a decade, Banks is still instantly recognisable; if he isn't America's greatest living artist, then surely, at six foot ten inches, he must be America's tallest living artist.

I jumped out of my car and intercepted him as he picked up a shopping cart on his way into the mall. As I approached him I introduced myself and showed him my credentials. He barged past me, and made a dash for the door of the mall. However, before he turned I managed to take a photograph, which, as I have mentioned, would have been the first of Mr Banks for several years. I say would, because that photograph was never developed.

Mr Banks disappeared into the mall and I was just about to follow him when he suddenly reappeared in the doorway in front of me, carrying a box of tomatoes. I halted and raised my camera to take another photograph; as I did a tomato landed at my feet. I looked up just in time to see another whistle past my nose. As I turned to run for the safety of my car I was struck on the right ear and I fell to the ground, dazed. Mr Banks ran up to me, grabbed my camera and smashed it on the ground, before stamping on it repeatedly for good measure. While he was distracted I seized my opportunity and made good my escape by car.

Since this incident Dave Hitzker has suffered recurring headaches, dizzy spells, and balance problems; he has yet to return to full-time work. Pending legal action resulting from the attack prevents him saying more at this time.

I'd found him. There was no doubt. A little hummingbird of excitement fluttered in my chest. Joseph Banks. I returned to the search page and hit the second link. It was to a site called The Contemporary Art Index.

I scrolled through; the page contained a short biography of Banks:

Joseph Banks 1943–
Conceptual Artist
Allied to no one movement, artistic or intellectual, Banks is one of American art's true originals; a pioneer in the field of conceptual art. Working in a multiplicity of media his work implicitly subverts re-emergent reactionary tropes, critiquing and de-reifying the normative and hegemonic structures usually associated with romantic notions of artist, authority and creativity, an approach exemplified in his later automatic pieces.

In 1997 Banks announced that he was withdrawing from the art world, and has exhibited no new work since then. This move has, if anything, served to increase interest in his work.

His work is still exhibited at the Gallery of Modern

Art in San Francisco, the Baltimore Gallery and the
Guggenheim in New York, amongst others.

After I read that I started to get quite a bad headache.
As I waited for the pages to print I tried to piece together
the implications of what I'd just found out. As far as I
could see, it seemed to suggest that the otter was a copy
of an original piece of Joe Banks art. But why had Banks
arranged for a copy to be made?

I was sitting in the big leather seats in the main bit of
Narita Airport, quietly nodding off, when someone called
my name.

'Felixsshh, ish zhat you?'

I sat up, rubbed my eyes and looked around. It was
Dennis. He was standing in front of me, a camera with
the biggest lens I've ever seen in my life hung around
his neck.

'Dennis . . . what are you doing here?' I asked, which
on the face of it was a pretty stupid question. I mean,
he's a plane spotter and it was an airport. Still, I thought
he was in Hong Kong for the fortnight.

'Fog, Felix, fog forecast for Chep Lap Kok, I flew out
just in time. Fog is the biggest enemy of the plane spotter
. . . but what are you doing here Felix?'

After I finished recounting my adventures, Dennis shook
his head.

'Felix, this is a very unusual story. Can I see this . . .
statue?'

I dug it out of my bag and handed it to him. He sat
for a while, looking at it closely, saying nothing. The fur
of the otter glistened in the light.

'Well, yes it is . . . how to say . . . most strange,' he said handing it back to me. 'So what do you do now?'

'I've got two options, I can either get on my flight back to Hong Kong, which leaves in three hours' time and then fly home, or I can spend more money and head off to the States, but there's no guarantee I'll find anything else out there.'

To tell the truth, I'd pretty much decided to sack it and head home. I'd checked the balance on the account and found that I'd already spent over £1,800, plus I only had the sketchiest of leads in the States.

Dennis frowned.

'Yeah, I know, you must think I'm mad,' I said hastily.

'No, not at all. Anyway, you should not worry about what other people think. For example, most people, probably including you, think I'm crazy . . .'

I made to protest.

'No Felix, be honest, I do not care.'

I shrugged. 'OK, maybe I think you're a little mad,' I said smiling, to indicate that I meant it in a good kind of way.

'And Felix, you may be correct . . . but I do not care. It is what I enjoy,' he said returning my smile. 'I think, Felix, that you have come this far, you should see it to the end.'

'But the cost . . . I'm in deep trouble as it is.'

'Can I see your tickets?' asked Dennis. I rummaged in my bag, pulled out the tickets and handed them to him. He studied them for a minute. 'OK Felix, I think I can do something about this,' he said standing up, 'just wait there,' he said over his shoulder as he headed off in the direction of the airline check-in desks.

Which is how, about thirty minutes later, my flights back to Hong Kong and the UK had been cancelled and transferred to a one-way flight into LAX with a transfer to San Francisco and then an onward flight home to the UK with a short stopover in Newark. All for an extra £200. How the motherfucker pulled it off I don't know, but I guess he used some of his mad plane-related skillz. After the ticket was sorted I thanked Dennis about a million times until he got heartily sick of it.

'Felix,' he said, looking a little exasperated, 'if you want to thank me, buy me some lunch. I am hungry.'

I've only eaten sushi a couple of times before and then only from the supermarket, so I have to say I felt pretty cool as I sat on my stool, contemplating the surreal parade of dishes gliding past me on the brushed metal mobius strip type conveyor device. Dennis didn't hang around and went straight for a plate of raw salmon. I watched as he deftly manoeuvred one of the fleshy pink slabs into his mouth.

'I thought you were vegetarian,' I said, remembering his request on the plane to Hong Kong.

'No.'

'But on the plane . . .'

'Oh, yes,' he laughed, 'I always eat vegetarian food on planes, often it is very much nicer. If you fly many times, you learn these things.'

I turned back to the sushi. Dennis carefully lifted what looked like a plate of tuna off the conveyor and tucked in. The sushi all looked so perfect, it seemed a shame to eat any.

'Aren't you hungry?' asked Dennis, spooning some

181

popped blisters of pickled ginger onto his plate. 'Here, have one of these,' he continued, lifting a plate off the conveyor and placing it between us.

I picked up my chopsticks and slipped them out of the paper cover. They were joined at the top by a small bridge of wood and came apart with a percussive snap. I slipped them between my fingers and picked up one of the pieces of sushi.

'What do you do, Dennis?' I asked, adjusting the slightly precarious tower of empty plates in front of me.

'How do you mean?'

'As a job . . . you know, when you're not plane spotting.'

'I see,' he said, pausing to wipe his lips with a serviette, 'I am an engineer.'

'Do you work with planes?'

'No, I am a civil engineer. I work on flood defences.'

'But you never fancied actually working with planes?' I asked.

Dennis looked at me. 'People are always asking me this question . . .' he said thoughtfully, 'and I always say the same reason.' I looked at him expectantly. He paused. 'Because planes are like dreams.'

I was like, 'What the fuck are you talking about?'

'I have always loved planes, from when I was a young boy I thought them to be . . . how would you say, like magic.'

'Magical,' I suggested.

Dennis nodded. 'They are magical things. It is just one hundred years and what they can do in this time . . . the amazing engineering, the thoughts of many people over the whole of human history, people who have thought about gravity, about aerodynamics, about navigation. They take you above the clouds and then put you down a little later somewhere completely different . . . like in a dream . . . I am sorry, for me, it is not so easy to talk like this in English.' He lost me a bit with the dreams thing, but I think I got the point.

'But that still doesn't explain why you don't work with them.'

'I have thought about this many times and I think the best answer is to say I didn't want to spoil the dream. I think if I worked for them then maybe they would not be dreams any more. Also, what I do is important, over twenty-five per cent of the Netherlands is under sea level, if no one maintained the dykes and waterways the country would be . . . how would you say . . . inundated?'

Anyway, after that Dennis shot the shit about planes for some time. Like it got a bit technical and boring, but I let him rattle on, because it would have been massively churlish to do otherwise, particularly seeing as he'd just sorted me out with my tickets. Plus, when it came time to pay for the sushi he totally wouldn't let me.

The US immigration official was a balding, flabby man with a bushy moustache and piggy eyes. He bore more than a passing resemblance to the man in the statue he held to his ear.

'It's not a bomb,' I said, sitting back in my chair and folding my arms.

He glared at me and raised his index finger to his lips.

When he was satisfied that it wasn't ticking, he placed the statue back on the table and sat down.

'Mike, what do you think?' he said, turning to his similarly lardiferous colleague.

'Well Drew, technically speaking, it's a heavy, blunt object. It could be used to assault a member of staff and seize control of the plane.'

I tried to imagine the scene. A mid-air struggle, me bludgeoning the captain with the otter.

'It's not a bomb and it's not a weapon either,' I said forcefully, 'I mean, do I look like a terrorist?'

Mike sucked in his cheeks. 'Terror has many different faces.'

'Sorry, let me get this clear, you think Osama Bin Laden has been recruiting English schoolboys to undertake suicide missions on the US armed only with—'

'Kid, don't get smart with us,' interrupted Mike, 'this is a serious business. Lives are at stake every day. We're the thin line that protects America from its enemies.'

As I reflected that they probably ate too many doughnuts to be considered a thin line, Mike's walkie-talkie buzzed. He stood up and answered. 'Yeah . . . but what about the obscenity aspect? What does the super say?' Mike stepped outside.

A couple of minutes later he stuck his head round the door and called Drew out, leaving me on my own with the statue.

I looked around the room. It was a blank, faceless place, with beige walls and worn grey carpet tiling on the floor. One of the two small security cameras mounted on the walls swung round and focussed on me. As I looked down at the floor, away from the camera, I noticed a large dark stain spreading out from under the table. I prodded it with my foot, but it was dry. Still, it looked pretty fresh. I wondered what it was. Had Mike just spilt the coffee he drank with his doughnuts? Or was it something more sinister?

I started to feel a little nervous. Who else had been locked up in this room before me, and what for? What had happened here, what atrocities had been recorded by the unblinking eye of the camera?

As I stared at the stain it struck me that my fate lay in the hands of these fat, humourless agents of the state. If they wanted I'd be wearing a pointy hood and standing on a box with wires attached to my goolies. OK, so maybe I exaggerate, but at the time the thought was pretty scary.

I looked over at the statue. The otter smiled back at

me with the same fixed grin as if it were mocking me. Mocking my plight.

Fortunately, it was not long before Mike reappeared bearing good news. 'OK kid, we're going to let you go this time, seeing as you've got an onward flight to the UK booked, but,' he added, scratching his distended gut, 'you better watch your step, we're logging your details on our database and you put one foot out of line . . .'

I had to run like a hell to catch my connection to San Francisco, which I made with only a few minutes to spare on account of my dealings with the US's vanguard in its war against terror.

By the time I got into San Francisco, at around 5.00 p.m., I was totally wiped out. In fact, I felt so terrible that I couldn't face getting the subway, so I decided that I would treat myself to a taxi instead. After getting a hundred dollars out of the cash machine, I found the taxi rank and slithered into the back of a cab. Where I pretty much crashed. I felt all hollow and empty inside, like my pulpy innards had been scooped out and thrown in the bin and there was just a little candle guttering in my chest leaving sooty marks on the inside of my cranium.

Whatever.

I'd never been to the US, but as I looked out of the window of the cab I started to get this bizarre feeling that I'd been there before. It was a bit like déjà vu; however, unlike déjà vu, which disappears as soon as you try to pin it down, this feeling persisted. It was pretty disconcerting. As I tried to work out what was happening a black and white police car whooped by, like it was on the tail of the Blues Brothers, and it occurred to me that everything was familiar because I had been there before. In about a million Hollywood films.

As I hadn't managed to score a guidebook, I got the cab to drop me outside a likely-looking hotel right in the centre of town, a couple of blocks away from this big skyscraper/pyramid building which looked like it was about to take off into space at any moment with some supervillain at the controls.

The hotel was pretty expensive; the cheapest available room was seventy dollars, but I was in desperate need of somewhere to crash, so I didn't object. Plus, the receptionist was a total fox. She was in her mid-twenties, with long blonde hair and a lean, lightly tanned body. I smiled as I handed her my bank card. She returned the smile as she swiped the card. The machine bleeped and she looked down at the screen. Then, without blinking, she reached below the counter, pulled out the biggest pair of motherfucking scissors I have ever seen in my entire life and deftly cut my card in two, right in front of me. There was nothing I could do.

'Whaa . . . what are you doing?'

'I'm sorry sir, this card is no longer valid,' she said with this smug little look on her face. Like you could totally tell this was a major highlight in her pathetic little life.

'But I just took some money out in the airport . . .'

'Unfortunately sir, the machine reports an irregular spending pattern for this card. You'll have to contact the issuer.' Which was not an option: there was no way I could contact the issuer without my mother getting involved.

'But . . . I . . . I've got no more money, I'm . . . where am I going to sleep?'

'You could always try People's Park.'

'What?'

'It's in Berkeley; it's where homeless people sleep.'

'I can't sleep there,' I said angrily.

'Sorry sir, but I'm going to have to ask you to leave,' she said, waving to someone behind me. I turned to see this puffed-up doorman in a green and gold uniform bearing down on me. I was like 'OK, OK, I'm, going.'

Outside the hotel, I stood wondering what to do, still a little uncomprehending of the whole situation on account of my jet lag. The doorman glared at me. I stood my ground and returned his stare. He stepped away from the door towards me. I started walking. He stopped and watched as I walked a little further, then turned and flipped him the Vs before charging off down the hill. When I was satisfied he wasn't chasing me I stopped. For about a minute I felt quite elated, but as I calmed down it occurred to me that (a) he probably didn't even know what the Vs were, and (b) I was now homeless and penniless in San Francisco.

OK, I wasn't quite penniless because I still had around fifty dollars left after paying for the taxi from the airport, but still, I wasn't in a good position.

After a little consideration I decided that I needed to check my e-mail and work out what to do next, so I went on the hunt for an internet cafe. It didn't take me long to find one, it being San Francisco.

It was pretty smart. A row of flat screen monitors lined the glass frontage, large multicoloured plastic tubes hung from the roof and in the centre of the room several twenty-somethings wearing expensive grey and black threads sat in these huge leather sofas, staring dreamily into the screens of their laptops. I hesitated for a second; it looked like it might be a bit pricey, but I needed to check my mail so I pushed open the door and walked in.

At the counter, a young man, dressed in the same smart black clothes as his customers greeted me.

'How are you today, sir?' he asked cheerily, as if I went there every day.

'Fine,' I replied automatically.

'What can I do to help you?'

'Um . . . I'd like to use the internet for a few minutes if that's possible,' I said, picking up this tourist map of the city from a plastic holder by the till.

'OK, just take a seat sir and I'll bring over your coffee,' said the counter guy. I just stood there looking vacantly at the map. 'It's free,' said the counter guy helpfully.

I looked up, perplexed.

'The map . . . it's free . . . the map's free.'

'Oh, yeah . . . right sorry, I'm a little jet-lagged,' I said, by way of explanation.

'I thought you sounded like you're from out of town.'

'Yeah, I just flew in from Japan, I'm still feeling a little . . . disorientated.'

'OK, you just sit down and I'll get your coffee. Let's see if we can beat that jet lag.' He was really friendly and polite in a way that you'd never get back home. If I'd have been in the UK he'd have sneered and grunted and then gone out the back and whipped me up some of his own special man-latte.

As I waited for my coffee, I checked my mail. After Dennis had sorted out my tickets to San Francisco I'd mailed Jim to keep him up to date with my movements.

When I opened my mail I found he'd replied:

RE: One Nite in Paris Bit torrent
Yo,
By the time you read this I guess you'll be in San Francisco. Mind you it wouldn't surprise me to find out that you are in fact holed up in Wolver-fucking-hampton or something and making all of this up. Seriously though, have you met any hotties yet? I reckon even you've got a chance in San Francisco what with all the men being otherwise engaged. Anyway, I just finished my first day at Violet's and I have to say that I can't understand why you hate her so much. She's a good laugh, plus she's paying me fifteen quid a day and she got some beers in.

In other news: Vespasian is doing pretty well and should be back on his feet in a couple days. Which is good because Violet was very worried and the dog means a great deal to her.

Jim
p.s. please get your sister to call the hounds off. Being followed around by a group of thirteen-year-old girls is deeply embarrassing and people might get the wrong idea.

I was like, 'Violet? Fifteen quid? Beer? Has the world gone mad?' If I hadn't had other things on my mind I might have been a little pissed off. Mind you, it was good news that Vespasian was on the road to recovery. I was still feeling massively guilty about the whole thing.

*

The day after Vespasian ate the Z, I finally beat Mrs P at Scrabble. She sat and glowered at me as I tidied the board away. The wrinkles of her face scrunched up into tightly packed isobars of fury.

I was a gracious winner and refused to gloat, but only because I knew it would wind her up even more.

'Well done Felix,' she said through gritted teeth, 'I can see I am having a good influence on you – though of course that wasn't an official win,' she said, simultaneously trying to take credit for my victory yet discrediting its validity in one fell swoop.

'What do you mean, not an official win?' I said, losing my cool.

'The Z is missing.'

'I know . . . but it's the same for both of us.'

'Yes, well, that's as maybe, but it still doesn't count.'

'Why?'

'Well it would be like two chess players playing a game, each with a pawn missing. It may be even for them, but it wouldn't count as a real game of chess.'

I was outraged. I'd beaten her fair and square and yet here she was snatching back my victory.

'I suggest if you want to win a proper game you find that Z post-haste,' she continued, the contours of her face relaxing into a smug smirk.

And that's why I gave Vespasian the laxatives. I figured

it would flush out the missing Z so I could kick her ass good and proper. I figured it would teach them both a lesson.

*

As I sat and thought about my next steps, the counter guy reappeared.

'Hi, would you like a refill?'

'Oh, yeah, sure,' I replied absent-mindedly, handing him my empty coffee cup, 'you wouldn't happen to know the cheapest way to get to Puerto Novo would you?'

'Puerto Novo,' he said thoughtfully, 'that's up the coast, right?' I nodded.

'Yeah . . . it would have to be the Greyhound, if you really want the cheapest, I'd say you'd get a return for around thirty or forty dollars.'

'Is there a bus tonight?' I asked.

He shrugged, 'I don't know, but if you want you could check their website.'

It took me a couple of minutes to find the timetable; the news wasn't good. The last bus of the day that stopped at Puerto Novo had already gone, and the next one didn't leave until 8.14 a.m. the following day. Which meant I now had a catch-22-type problem. I could try and find a hostel for the night, but if I did I wouldn't be able to afford the bus. If I wanted to track down Joe Banks and discover more about the statue, I'd have to spend the night on the streets of San Francisco. It occurred to me that I could stay the night in a hostel and then try to hitchhike up the coast in the morning. But I discounted that idea. I'd seen enough slasher flicks to know that hitchers in the US are like some sort of prey species.

The counter guy returned with the second cup of

coffee; as I sat and drank it I considered my final option: throwing in the towel and phoning my mother. I reckoned she'd be able to pay for a hotel room for me; you've got no idea how valuable a warm bed and a safe place to sleep is until it's taken away from you. But I knew if I phoned my mother, it would be the end of my journey.

A big sign in the shape of a ship's wheel informed me I was in Fisherman's Wharf. Crowds of deeply uncool plump people, all dressed in polo shirts, khaki shorts and sports sandals, waddled around the shops and stalls which sold Hopi ear candles, reproduction 'antique' puppets and other items indispensable to the average fisherman. As I surveyed the scene a large woman with a derelict face appeared through the crowd. She was pushing a supermarket trolley overflowing with dirty plastic bags full of god knows what. The crowd of shoppers parted to let her through, disgust etched on their faces. She stopped and started frantically scratching her arms, first one, then the other, as she muttered some deranged spell.

I looked at the revulsion on the faces of the people around her and it made me sick. I felt so sorry for her, and so angry at all the people around me. They were so rich and she had nothing. They'd happily spend a hundred dollars on an aromatherapy gift pack or whatever, but wouldn't even give the woman a buck. It sucked. I mean, I would have given her something myself, but I only had about fifty dollars left and I still wasn't sure what I was going to do.

OK, so maybe I was being a bit harsh. I was jet-lagged and lonely, plus I was feeling pretty freaked about what I was going to do that night. And I suppose when it comes down to it, it's not like you can help everyone in the world, can you?

As I headed back up the hill into town, it started to get dark. I briefly considered finding somewhere to sleep in the garden of one of the big houses that lined the street, but then I thought that if I was asleep anything could happen and phrases like 'dismembered body parts', 'plastic bags' and 'several locations around the city' started to drift through my head so I canned the idea.

I also contemplated heading down to the bus station, but then I remembered that every major bus station I'd ever been in had been a total hive of scum and villainy, so I nixed that idea too. In the end I decided to try and find a bar or cafe that was open late. If that wasn't an option I'd just keep walking and stay awake.

I checked the map I picked up in the internet cafe and decided to head back to the centre of town. I wandered back over to Market Street into Soma and the Mission, where it was still busy, full of people enjoying themselves. I made to walk into a bar. A big man in a cut-off Guns 'n' Roses T-shirt held his arm up and stopped me.

'ID.'

I dug in my pocket and handed him my passport. He looked at it.

'Sorry kid, but you have to be twenty-one to drink in this state.' What a bunch of primitives. Can you imagine that, twenty-one before you can have a beer? And they wonder why their children take so many drugs.

Whatever.

A little further down the same street, I found a small Lebanese restaurant which was open until 1.00 a.m. I ordered some falafel, the cheapest thing on the menu.

As I sat picking at my food, I read back over this diary. It's a funny thing, but up until that point, I'd been too involved in the whole thing to do a great deal of reflection. As I read I was struck by how much had happened. Only a week and a half before I'd been working in Mrs P's garden. Since then I'd travelled three quarters of the way around the world only to find myself homeless in San Francisco. It was all pretty random.

The falafel guy kicked me out at 1.00 on the dot and I wandered back up the hill past the sneering façades of the big Victorian mansions on Nob Hill (no giggling at the back). I figured that the posh residential part of town was a safer place to be.

At this point I was on what must have been about my fourth wind, but it didn't last too long and, as I walked, fear and tiredness closed in on me. I couldn't think straight. I started fantasising about meeting a couple of hippies or beatniks, and how they'd invite me to a poetry reading or a happening, and how when we got there someone would pass me a jug of wine and a joint, and how there'd be this beautiful girl with the sweetest smile and how our souls would make this immediate connection so we wouldn't even have to talk before we started kissing. How we'd end up balling in her soft eiderdown bed on her houseboat in the bay. How we'd be woken by her cat in the morning, with the sunlight streaming in the window . . .

Unfortunately, I started getting a boner which made walking difficult, so I made myself stop thinking about free love and all that other shit.

That night, time passed more slowly than I ever believed it could. I met no one as I trudged wearily round the streets of Nob Hill. At one point a police car slowed down as it passed. I could see the policeman in the passenger seat craning his neck to get a good look at me, but he obviously concluded that I didn't merit further investigation as they didn't stop.

I was a stumbling wreck as the cold, grey fingers of the new day eventually crept over the horizon and banished the demons and nightcrawlers back to their foul nests. The sky lightened quickly, but it was an overcast morning; low, grey bank of clouds hung over the city. I wandered away from Nob Hill, dragging myself through the empty streets in the direction of the Golden Gate Bridge.

When I got there I sat down on a park bench and looked over the narrow mouth of the bay at the scabby, rust-red coloured bridge. In the dull morning light it looked anything but golden.

Then I must have nodded off for a little while, because I woke with a start to find a man sitting next to me. The first thing I noticed was a band of tinsel wrapped around his head like a slipped halo.

'I hate you,' he said matter-of-factly.

Oh, fuck, I thought, this is it. My body tensed, ready to jump off the bench. I squinted into the lemony early morning light. The guy looked like he was around fifty, maybe a little older; though it's pretty hard to tell with homeless people. His face was thin and battered. Lank grey hair hung limply over the collar of his manky red puffa jacket. On his feet he wore two odd trainers, one Nike and one Adidas, showing a flagrant disregard for the concept of brand loyalty. At his feet sat a dirty green army-issue duffel bag. As I looked at him I wondered if I was still dreaming.

'I hate you,' he repeated calmly.

'Well I hate you too,' I replied, unsure of what else to say.

Apparently this was the right answer.

'You got it buddy, that's the goddamned truth, and you know it is,' he said, before standing up and breaking into a maniacal cackle. My brain felt raw and a little broken on that bench as I watched him wander off, dragging his bag behind him.

I got to the bus station at 7.00 a.m. It was quiet. Bleary-eyed people stood in silence, reading papers, drinking coffee. I sat down to wait. By 8.00 the station was busier, the people more animated, purposeful. I, on the other hand, felt even more shit. I just wanted to get on board the bus, get my seat, fall asleep and wake up in Puerto Novo.

When the bus pulled into the bay, the driver sat inside for about ten minutes, reading his paper and blatantly ignoring us, like we were some kind of subhuman scum. Eventually he folded his paper, opened the doors and let us on.

I found my seat, propped my rucksack against the window and settled down to sleep. The driver started gunning his engine, and I had just convinced myself that I'd managed to secure a double seat so I could spread out and snooze in comfort when this young guy in a baseball cap jumped on board. He stood for a second at the top of the aisle scanning the seats before striding up in my direction and sitting down next to me. And I wasn't about to say anything, because he was big, not particularly tall, but wide and bulgy. You could see he'd done a shitload of working out. As he sat down he nodded and pushed his baseball cap back on his head.

'Hey, there,' he said, 'name's Scott, where you headed for?'

'Er, Puerto Novo.'

'Hey, you're not American. Where you from?'

'I'm from the UK.'

'You're kidding! Man that's cool, I've always wanted to go there and see the Queen.'

I nodded and looked out of the window.

The bus pulled out of the station and joined the traffic surging north over Golden Gate Bridge. The day had brightened, I looked out of the bus window. Sharp, white commas of sail punctuated the brilliant, blue water of the bay.

'Sorry man, I didn't catch your name,' said Scott.

'Felix, the name's Felix,' I replied, turning to face him.

'Felix,' he repeated thoughtfully, 'well, pleased to meet you Felix.' He paused. 'How old are you?'

'Sixteen.'

'No shit, same here,' he said, readjusting his baseball cap. He was fucking big for sixteen. 'Where you say you were going again?'

'Up north. A small town called Puerto Novo.'

'Never heard of it,' he reflected. 'I'm headed for Seattle, my sister's up there. I'm moving in with her.'

'You been living in San Francisco?'

'Well, I guess you could say that,' he said, smiling wryly, 'yeah, been in a juvenile detention centre for the last three years. Got out yesterday.' And all I wanted was a nice quiet ride up to Puerto Novo, so I could catch up on my sleep.

I edged a glance at him, he was staring straight at the back of the headrest of the seat in front of him, chomping on his gum like a motherfucker.

'Know why I was inside?' he asked, still staring at the headrest. I shook my head. 'Stabbed a man with a screwdriver,' he said with a certain hint of pride in his voice, like he was telling me he'd come second in a monster-truck race or something. I was like, 'Oh fuck.' I was not up for dealing with a four hour bus ride with a protein-gorged, homicidal maniac. But I didn't really feel like I could tell him to shut the fuck up seeing as he'd just told me that he'd stabbed a man.

'Yeah, bastard tried to molest me. He was the warden at my children's home, tried it on with most of the kids, eventually he got round to me. His fucking mistake,' he said perfunctorily, his story stripped back to the bare facts.

'What happened to him?' I asked hesitantly, deciding I couldn't politely ignore him any longer.

'Nothing. He denied it all, ended up being my word against his. The judge believed him.'

'Doesn't that bother you?'

He stopped chewing his gum, turned and looked at me intensely. 'Yeah, a little, but I got my own life to lead now. All of that shit . . . it's in my past.'

'But . . . that's pretty fucking unfair,' I said shaking my head.

'Fair, unfair, it's all the same. Shit happens, you get over it,' he said, chewing his gum with renewed vigour. I looked out of the window again; we'd crossed the bridge, swept along into the middle of a great river of cars, haemorrhaging out of the city. Scott must have taken

202

this as some sort of sign that I was a bit freaked out or something.

'I didn't mean to spook you,' he said, a note of concern in his voice, 'I've had a lot of counselling . . . and he *was* trying to molest me . . .'

'Yeah, I'm sure,' I replied, trying to sound positive, but somehow it came out in a semi-flippant, negative kind of way.

'No really, Felix, there were other ways to solve that problem without stabbing him. I've been given a second chance.' He stopped and pulled a pack of Juicy Fruit out of his top pocket and offered me a stick. I refused. He shrugged, unwrapped a stick, spat the gum he was chewing into the paper and popped the new stick into his mouth.

Big, soft, fluffy clouds drifted by. I felt so tired, they looked so comfortable. The desire to sleep was so strong, but Scott wasn't finished.

'I'm going to be a psychic in Seattle.'

I was like, 'Is that something you can become?'

'Yeah, pretty neat little number,' he continued, 'my sister does it already.'

'She's psychic too?' I asked tentatively.

Scott laughed, 'Shit no, it's just easy to get into. You get this handbook from the company with the answers to pretty much any question you could think of. All you need's a phone.'

I nodded.

'Yeah,' he said, 'my sister says there's a real trick to it, because the company offers a cheap-rate call for like four minutes and when that's up this real premium rate kicks in and that's when you start making the big bucks.'

'Ah,' I said, knowingly.

'Yeah, it's a pretty sweet opportunity. My sister's earning close on a thousand a week. Life throws you lots of opportunities, all you gotta do is recognise them, and then act on them,' he said. Which, along with several other of his pronouncements, sounded suspiciously like something he had learned in one of his counselling sessions.

As the landscape rolled by, Scott talked more about Seattle and about being a phone psychic. I guess he was just happy to be out, able to talk. And actually, he seemed an OK sort of a dude. Anyway, before I knew it we'd reached Mendocino.

Now, I remember pulling out of Mendocino, but then I must have fallen asleep, because the next thing I remember is waking up with someone shaking me; it was Scott.

'Hey, Felix, it's Puerto Novo, c'mon, the driver's about to pull out.'

I struggled to my feet, still half asleep. I squeezed past Scott and stumbled down the aisle. The driver glared at me as I stepped down onto the kerb. The doors snapped shut behind me with an angry hiss.

As I stood and watched the bus wend its way slowly round the square, it suddenly hit me: I'd left my fucking rucksack on the bus. A tsunami of panic ripped through my body, but I just stood there, transfixed, seemingly incapable of action. Then, as the bus pulled onto the road north, it lurched to a sudden halt, the air brakes squealing a loud complaint. The doors opened and Scott appeared on the steps waving at me. I snapped out of my trance and ran towards the bus.

'There you go Felix,' he said, smiling as he handed me my rucksack.

'Come on kid, I've got to get this fucking show on the road,' said the bus driver impatiently. Scott ignored him.

'Have a good one my man,' he said holding his hand out for a high five, which I made.

'And you. I hope it all goes well for you up in Seattle,' I replied as the doors closed and the bus pulled away.

I sat down on a wooden bench at the edge of the square and composed myself. It wasn't like there was anything of any value in my rucksack, but I needed the otter. I needed it to show to Banks, to see what he knew about it. Plus it had a certain sentimental value: we'd been through a lot together.

Whatever.

The late-morning sun shone brightly on the town. Squat cliffs studded with white, wooden-fronted houses ringed the bay. A marina full of sleek pleasure yachts hugged the shore to the south while a few small fishing boats bobbed up and down in the middle of the bay, tugging playfully at their brightly coloured mooring buoys. I pulled out the copy of the article about Banks I'd printed. I read it slowly looking for clues. It identified his house as being just north of the town set back a little from the highway, and I was just about to head off and try and find the road when I realised that I was pretty hungry. I emptied my pockets. I had $5.20 left.

In the convenience store just off the square I bought a tuna wrap, a couple of cans of Coke, a big bag of Doritos and a small bag of Skittles. I sat back down on the bench and ate the wrap, then I stuffed the rest of the food into my rucksack and headed north.

The road skirted the shore before zigzagging up onto the cliff top, where a group of seagulls hung motionless, languidly riding the thermals which ran up the cliff face. The shittiness of the night before seemed a distant memory. I started to feel insanely free. I mean, I was on the other side of the world from home, with about a dollar left in my pocket, following some absurd, made-up quest and probably faced with a very awkward phone call to make to my mother explaining how I'd just blown several thousand pounds and was now stranded penniless in northern California. But, just then, I felt like my life couldn't get any better. The earth seemed to spin beneath my feet, like I was walking on a travelator in an airport or something. I felt one hundred per cent ebullient.

About two miles after the road reached the top of the cliff it swung inland, before descending sharply into a wooded valley. The wind dropped in the shelter of the large pine trees and the sun poured down from the cloudless sky.

At the bottom of the valley a small, rusty iron bridge crossed a shallow stream. I stood on the bridge and watched a group of fish flitting in the shadows below. It was quiet. Peaceful. Looking into the cool, clear water of the stream made me feel a little thirsty so I sat down and opened a can of Coke, dangling my legs between the spars of the bridge.

As I sat there idly watching the fish, a car suddenly appeared from the forest about fifty yards away, back in the direction from which I had just come. It was an old Volvo. It turned up the hill and drove away from me, towards town.

I was like, 'A Volvo. Fuck. Banks.' I jumped to my feet

and ran back up the hill to where the car had exited the forest and sure enough there was a narrow dirt road which I'd missed on my way down. It was well disguised, tree branches carefully arranged over the entrance so that if you weren't really looking you'd never see it. I stooped a little and pushed my way through. After a couple of steps the road opened out in front of me, winding off into the forest.

After ten minutes walk I came to a fork in the road. I tried to work out which way to go, but I could see nothing other than trees and track. I felt like I was in one of those *Sword and Sorcery* adventure books I had as a kid, where it goes like:

> you reach a fork in the road, to take the right fork turn to page 49 or to take the left fork turn to page 177

and if you turn one way you get stung to death by these mutant flying antzombies and if you turn the other way you meet this totally hot female elf.

I squatted down and examined the hard-packed dirt of the road surface. There were what seemed like fresh tyre tracks going in either direction. Both roads looked identical. I held my breath and listened, but the forest was quiet apart from the occasional bird call and the soft shushing of the wind in the tops of the trees.

In the absence of any clues about the direction of Banks's house, I decided to leave the decision to fate. I tossed a coin. As I lifted my hand I saw it was tails. I slipped the coin back into my pocket and started down the left-hand fork.

After walking for what seemed like an eternity, the trees got thicker, their overhanging branches cutting out the light a little. My feet felt pretty sore. The road forked for a second time. This time there were no car tracks to the right, but some pretty fresh ones to the left. I decided to follow them.

As I walked I started to feel a little less confident; by now it was late afternoon and there was still no sign of the gate or the house or anything mentioned in the article. Soon the trees really started to close in and the road petered out into a track. I reached a little clearing and stopped. I realised that this was definitely wrong. I mean, he had a car. I hadn't really been thinking, my brain was still foggy from jet lag and lack of sleep the night before.

I turned back, but almost as soon as I did the path split in two again. I didn't remember it doing that so soon. I couldn't remember if I should take the left or the right. In the end I tossed a coin again, which led me to another fork I didn't recognise about a couple of hundred yards down the track. An uneasy feeling started simmering gently in my stomach.

About an hour and several more coin tosses later I gave up. I was totally and utterly lost. I sat down in a small glade and took stock of my situation. In my ruck-sack I had a can of Coke, half a family-sized packet of Doritos, a bag of Skittles, some minging clothes and a small statue of a fat, bald man sodomising a pink, glittery otter. Totally useless. No matches, no commando knife, no deku nuts, no nothing. I looked up at the sky. Big clouds soaked in the red of the dying sun staggered past like eviscerated sheep. I ate the rest of the Doritos.

When I got back up I decided to mark my trail with the Skittles. OK, so you're supposed to start from a known point . . . but I wasn't really thinking straight, so it seemed like a good idea at the time.

The forest became denser, then the trail disappeared altogether. I tried to retrace my steps but I couldn't find them, every way I turned the forest seemed to block me, the trees seemed bigger, older and more malevolent. Their twisted roots tripped me as I blundered on, briars tugged at my clothes and scratched my skin. I stopped again and tried to think. The forest was eerily quiet, even the birds I'd heard earlier had fallen silent.

I walked for another hour or so, until it started to get dark. I checked the bag of Skittles. There were only a few left, so I sat down and ate them. For about the fifty millionth time in the last two weeks I wondered how the fuck I got there. Lost in a forest in northern California. It was preposterous. I could die here I thought, and then maybe nobody would find my body for years, by which point I'd be just a pile of bleached bones lying at the bottom of a tree, alongside a statue of a pink, glittery otter being sodomised by a small, fat, bald man. OK, so it would have made a good episode of *The X-Files*, but it would have been a bit of a downer for me.

Whatever.

I decided to make camp where I was. By now it was a little cold so I put on the rest of my clothes. I ended up looking like I was on *South Park* and my other pair of jeans still had crispy puke all over them and stank pretty badly, which made me worry that the smell might attract bears or wolves or something. Though I wasn't even sure if you got bears and wolves in northern California.

While it had been light the forest had seemed like an all right place to be, full of nice little birds and squirrels and shit; now, all I could hear was snapping twigs, creaking branches and weird moaning noises. It sounded like there was some sort of haunted porno shoot going on. Then I started thinking about *Blair Witch* and *Evil Dead II* and other dark shit. Pretty quickly, I was so scared that every time I heard a new noise, I just about jumped out of my skin. I scanned the gloomy forest floor for a weapon, but I couldn't see anything. Then I remembered what the immigration official had said, so I sat down with my back to a tree, got the statue out of the bag and held the head of the otter in my hands like it was a baseball bat and waited for the bears, antzombies, spunkwraiths or whatever to show face.

When I woke, I looked up to see faint, early-morning light seeping down through the tops of the trees, and though I was still cold, hungry and lost, I never felt happier in my entire life.

After considering my situation for a little while, I remembered something from a survival programme I'd seen on the Discovery Channel where the presenter said that as a general rule, if you are lost anywhere in the world, walk downhill. As I remembered it the logic was that this would eventually lead you to water which would:

(a) keep you alive; and
(b) probably lead you to civilisation.

So that's what I did. And I'll be fucked if it didn't work. I found this track that headed downhill and within an hour I found a stream with a little path running alongside it. After following the stream for about half an hour it led me to the bridge where I'd watched the fish the day before. I scrambled up the bank and onto the road, feeling pretty chuffed with myself, a feeling which was soon tempered by the realisation that I was really only back where I started.

I sat for fifteen minutes debating what to do. In no way did I want to repeat the experience of the night before, but then again, I wasn't going to give up at this point. I'd travelled round the world, gone through some pretty amazing shit and there was no way I could just give up at the last hurdle. My belly complained loudly at my decision. But I overruled it and decided to give it one more go.

I found the road entrance again and instead of taking the first left fork, I took the right. I walked about a mile down the track where my progress was halted by a large, wrought-iron gate set in a tall, chain-link fence topped with a vicious slinky of razor wire. I looked through the bars of the gate, but I couldn't see anything other than the track winding off into the forest.

An intercom was fixed to the left-hand gatepost below a picture of two slavering Rottweilers with a warning about the dangers of trespassing. I pressed the intercom button. Nothing happened. I waited. Nothing happened. I briefly considered trying to find a hole in the fence, but the picture of the dogs put me off. In the end I decided that the only thing to do was hang around and hope that Banks came back fairly soon.

I sat down with my back against the gate and started to write up this diary and I'd got to the end of my night in San Francisco when I started to feel drowsy.

When I woke my head felt tight and sore. Sun streamed down through the trees. Hot and befuddled by sleep, I looked up, straight into the vexed face of a Volvo staring at me.

'Hey, you, get out of my way,' said the driver.

I stood, holding up one hand as a shield against the sun which shone directly into my eyes.

'Mr Banks?' I asked, tentatively.

'No, never heard of him, now get out of my way or I'll call the sheriff.'

'It is you . . . isn't it?'

'No . . . look it doesn't matter if it's me or not, I'm sick of people coming out here and stalking me. I don't care who you are, if you're a journalist from the *New York Times* or a grad student from Berkeley, I'm not saying anything.'

'I'm not a grad student, I'm still at school. My name is Felix.'

'You an Englishman?'

'Yeah.'

'Don't get many English schoolboys trying to track me down, that's for sure,' he said, slightly less aggressively.

'Oh, so you *are* Joe Banks?'

'Yes, I suppose I am, but that doesn't change things, I'm still not talking.'

'But I've come a long way.'

'Sorry, I can't help that. It was your decision to come here, not mine.'

212

'Look,' I said, bending down and rummaging in my rucksack, struggling a little to get the statue out.

'Drop, it, drop the fucking bag now, and put you hands on your head.' I looked up and froze. Banks was standing by the car, pointing a handgun right at me. He looked like the description in the paper, tall, with long white hair. And when I say tall, I mean absolutely massive. The man was a giant.

I let go of the bag and raised my hands. And you know what? My mobile phone went off.

Banks stood looking at me down the barrel of the pistol, which looked like a child's toy in his huge hands. 'Switch it off,' he said gruffly.

'It's in my . . . pocket,' I replied, indicating with my chin, my hands still clasped on top of my head.

'Take it out slowly and switch it off,' he said, stepping a little closer. I removed the phone from my pocket, and as I did, I looked at the display: it was my mother. I was like, 'Sorry, mummy, can't talk, there's another man pointing a gun at me.'

I switched it off.

'OK, put the phone down on the hood of the car, along with the bag,' he said. I complied. 'Now, move away from the car.'

I stepped back a couple of paces. He leaned over and pulled the rucksack towards him. He opened the top a little and peered inside, still keeping the gun trained in my direction. Then suddenly he stood upright, letting the hand holding the gun drop to his side.

'Where in the name of God did you get this?' he said, looking at me.

*   *   *

Joe's pad was more of a log mansion than a log cabin. The rooms were all massive, with vaulted ceilings and smooth flagstone floors. Expensive modern furniture lounged around on Persian rugs. Modern art and African masks hung from the wooden walls. It was the kind of gaff that Jean Luc Picard hangs out in when he's on Earth leave in *Next Generation*.

'Look, I'm really sorry about the gun. I had a security audit done a couple of months ago and they recommended that I pull the gun first, ask questions later. I have some pretty odd fans out there . . .' said Joe apologetically.

'Don't worry,' I replied, 'really . . . I'm used to it,' which was probably stretching the truth a little, but it was the second time I'd had a gun pulled on me in the last two weeks, so I said it with some justification. Joe looked puzzled, but said nothing. 'Nice view,' I said, by way of small talk, looking out of the big patio doors, over a flower-filled meadow that ran down to the shore of a small lake.

Joe nodded. 'Would you like a beer?' he asked, walking over to the kitchen area.

'Er, yeah . . .'

'So tell me, Felix, where'd you find the otter?' said Joe, handing me one of the bottles, before taking a seat on one of the low sofas in the middle of the room. I sat down opposite and told him the whole thing. I told him about the House of Ming, then I told him about Hong Kong, Shenzhen, Cheng, Mr Huai, Tokyo, Miko and Mr Itabashi, San Francisco, getting lost in the wood . . .

When I finished he let out a long, low whistle. 'So

you've tracked this thing most of the way round the world?'

'Yep,' I said proudly.

'Wow, Felix, that's some adventure you've had,' he said thoughtfully. I shrugged, absently picking at the silver foil around the neck of my beer bottle. 'You must be hungry though, after last night. Do you need something to eat?'

'Yeah, sure, something to eat would be good,' I replied, trying not to sound too desperate, 'but what about the statue? Did you make it?'

Joe frowned. 'Look . . . sorry Felix, that's going to have to wait until I've fixed up the food.'

I lay back on the sofa, sinking into the soft cushions, cooking smells drifted across the room, my stomach groaned. I'd forgotten how hungry I was. A little while later Joe appeared carrying a couple of plates.

'Come on Felix, we'll eat on the deck,' he said, sliding open the patio doors with his foot. As I stood up I got a little head rush from the beer or the jet lag or the tiredness or whatever.

'I'm sorry, it's just a plain omelette,' said Joe. 'Anna, the maid, usually does the cooking, but she left a couple of days ago to visit family in Mexico City, so I'm on my own.' We sat in silence as we ate. The omelette tasted great. When we'd finished, I helped Joe clear away the dishes. While I loaded the dishwasher, Joe opened a bottle of red wine and poured himself a big glass.

Back on the deck we sat soaking up the heat of the late-afternoon sun.

'You know,' said Joe hesitantly, 'the otter was the last piece I ever made.' My heart skipped a beat. So it

215

was a piece of art; I couldn't wait to tell Jim that he was talking out of his tailpipe. 'Yeah, I think I made it in '97 . . . maybe early '98,' he continued, before draining his glass in one big gulp. The sun dipped down behind the trees and the temperature seemed to drop a couple of degrees. A shiver trickled down my spine. 'Let's go inside,' said Joe, 'you look like you're suffering a bit from your night in the forest. I take it you would like to stay the night?'

I nodded. 'Sure, if that's OK.'

'No problem,' said Joe, 'follow me.'

I was going to ask about the otter but I didn't say anything; I got the impression that it would be best to let him tell me about it in his own time.

Joe opened the door and ushered me into the bedroom, in the middle of which stood a king-size bed, which made me sleepy just by looking at it.

'Oh, yeah, Felix, if you want a shower, there's a bathroom down at the bottom of the hall and there's a towel over the chair, next to your bed.'

When Joe left I sat down on the edge of the bed and I was going to flop backwards onto it, but I knew if I did I'd probably sleep for the next year or something. Plus, the thought of a shower sounded pretty appealing. It was about three days since I'd had a proper wash, and I'd slept rough for the last two nights. My ming factor was off the scale.

There were two identical doors at the bottom of the corridor. As I stood there, holding my towel in place around my midriff, I tried to remember if Joe had said which one it was, but I couldn't. I pushed open the door on my right, but it wasn't the bathroom. It was an artist's studio.

In the centre of the room stood an easel, on which sat a nude portrait of a woman lying on this bed/sofa type thing. I stepped into the room and looked around. The walls were covered in pictures. Many more canvases were stacked on the floor, leaning against the walls. There must have been hundreds of them scattered around the room. I walked over to a pile and looked through them. And do you know what? All the pictures were of the same woman.

She looked to me as if she were around forty-five, maybe fifty. She had long blonde hair. In the picture on the easel she was smiling sadly. She looked weary, defeated, which was kind of a bit weird, because she was naked and everything. I mean, she had pretty big tits and a dark hairy muff, and as I stood staring at her I started to get a boner, which I admit is pretty fucked up on several different levels. Anyway, it totally creeped me out, standing there with a semi, dressed in nothing but a towel, being stared at by all those pictures of the same woman. I felt like I was maybe intruding on something very private, plus, I started shitting it that Joe might catch me and be angry, so I backed out of the room and closed the door.

I stayed in the shower for a long time, standing under the hot water as it washed away the grime of the last few days. I resisted the temptation to crack one off, despite the fact that I still kind of had the horn.

When I'd finished, I put on my least dirty set of clothes and made my way back to the living room, feeling a lot better. Joe was hunkered down on the big stone hearth, tending to a fire it looked as if he had just lit.

'How was your shower?' he asked, getting up and sitting down on one of the sofas.

'Good . . . great in fact,' I replied, sitting down opposite him. Joe looked at me and poured himself another big glass of wine from a freshly opened bottle that sat on the coffee table. He seemed to be fairly tearing through the booze.

'I've been thinking about your story Felix. Can I ask how much you paid for the statue in this store you were talking about?'

'Thirty . . . sorry £29.99.'

'What's that . . . about forty-five, fifty bucks?' asked Joe. I nodded; it seemed about right. 'Have you considered how much it might be worth?' he said, rolling the wine around in his glass.

'No . . . I haven't really thought. I didn't know it was worth anything more than what I paid for it,' I replied.

'Well Felix, I reckon that in today's market it's probably worth . . . what . . . a million . . . maybe even a million and a half.' I almost had a fucking prolapse. I picked up my beer, my hand shaking like I was some sort of strung-out basehead or something. I looked over at the fire; kindling spat and popped angrily as the yellow flames took hold.

'As in a million dollars?'

'Shocked?' said Joe, smiling wryly. I sat there dumbly clinging to my beer bottle. I just kept thinking about how I'd almost left the statue on the bus. How I'd carted the thing halfway round the world in my rucksack.

'Bbb . . . bbut how?' I stammered.

'It's a Joe Banks original. That's what they're worth,' said Joe.

218

'But I thought Miko's da . . . Mr Itabashi, I thought he made it?'

'He did.'

'But—'

'That's how I work Felix . . . or at least it's how I used to work. I'd come up with the idea and then get someone else to make it. It's not a novel concept, everyone from Rembrandt to Andy Warhol has used the same method. The statue you bought for fifty bucks is a one-off. I got Mr Itabashi to design it after I saw some of his netsuke in a gallery in Japan, then I got Mr Uko to engage Mr Huai's company to make a copy of Mr Itabashi's original.'

About fifty million thoughts were running through my head. I grabbed one and turned it into words.

'But why, why not use the original . . . why make a copy?'

'That was the point Felix, can't you see? A unique piece of art made using mass production techniques . . . it's ironic,' said Joe in an ironic kind of manner, before pouring himself more wine. I tried to order my thoughts.

'But how did it end up in the UK . . . in that shop?'

'That I don't know. But I do know that it was stolen about two years ago from the private collector I sold it to, and it's definitely the original. I made a secret mark on the base after I got it to make sure that Mr Huai's company didn't produce copies.'

'But Mr Huai . . . how come he didn't know it was valuable?'

'He never knew it was a piece of art. We told him it was a test piece for a range of ornaments. After the factory made the first one, we terminated the contract, paid the penalty clauses and smashed the mould. It was all over-seen by Mr Uko,' said Joe in a matter-of-fact kind of way, 'put it this way Felix, if Mr Huai knew what it was worth, I'm fairly sure it, and probably you, wouldn't be sitting here today.'

I took a deep breath. My hand was still shaking. When Joe said it was something he'd made earlier on I thought he meant it was a copy, not the original.

Joe stood up and disappeared into the kitchen, returning with a full bottle of whisky. He sat down and started fiddling with the stopper.

'So what happens now?' I asked.

'How do you mean?'

'Well . . . with the otter . . .'

'What, you want to know if you're rich?' asked Joe, frowning.

'No . . . I just wondered . . .' I said awkwardly, 'seri-ously Joe, I had no idea this was worth anything until you said just now . . .'

Joe looked at me intently.

'But . . . I mean . . . I didn't come to get money. I didn't know it was a piece of art.'

'Felix, it's a piece of shit, not a piece of art, can't you see?'

I was confused. First he tells me that it was a piece of art worth a million dollars or more, than he says it's a piece of shit. It didn't make sense. Joe poured himself a large whisky into the wine glass. The dregs of wine turned the whisky pale red.

'Honestly Joe, it's nothing to do with money.'

'Then why exactly are you here Felix?' asked Joe,

looking at the floor, before throwing back the whisky in one gulp.

'Well, it's like I said . . . I just happened to find the otter and then I got my mother's bank card—'

'No Felix, not how, why?' he said, a hint of impatience in his voice. It was a good question. The fire was now fully alight; heat spilled over the flagstones into the room.

'I don't know . . . I guess I thought it was pretty cool.'

'Cool,' said Joe with a dismissive snort, 'well thank you Felix, that's the ultimate accolade . . .'

'I suppose I just want to know what the statue is, what it means.'

'You want to know what it means?' Joe repeated deliberately. I nodded. 'It's always the fucking same, everyone who comes here wants me to tell them what my art means,' said Joe loudly, leaning over the table towards me. I was like, 'Oh shit.' I had evidently said the wrong thing.

I looked into the fire. The flames had taken hold on the bigger logs, yellow turned to orange, the flickering light danced on the walls, playing over the African masks which leered maliciously out of the gloom. I started to feel a little scared. I was in the middle of nowhere with some boozehound artist, who was acting in an increasingly random manner.

'What do *you* think it means Felix?' asked Joe in the same angry tone, picking up the bottle of whisky and raising it to his lips. He threw his head back and took several swift gulps. When he put the bottle back down on the table, it was less than half full. I could feel my heart beating like crazy. I looked nervously over at the coffee table; the statue seemed animated by the shifting light of the fire, it looked like the bald man was pumping away at the otter. I tried to think, but Joe didn't give me a chance to reply.

'I'll tell you what it means, Felix,' said Joe, pausing for effect. 'It means nothing. It's empty. Meaningless. My so-called art is utterly worthless, and that thing you found is the worst . . . a ham-fisted piece of trash . . . pathetic, childish irony.'

I said nothing. By this point I had decided it was the best policy. Joe was raving, it looked like he'd totally lost it.

'Felix,' he said, 'I look at the world and the way it's gone since I was young, in the late fifties, early sixties, I see all the things I fought for, marched for, created art about, all of it's been for nothing.' His voice slurred and choked with anger. 'All we've done is create a world where our only function is to produce and consume, a world where the rich have got richer, while the poor have got poorer, a world we're destroying for the sake of bigger SUVs and the right to have strawberries out of season, a world where the only meaning of my art is its commercial value, a world where God is dead . . . and where we don't give a shit.'

Joe got to his feet unsteadily and walked over to the fire where he bent down and picked up a large poker which lay on the hearth.

'My art is meaningless, worthless, it's had no impact, it's changed nothing,' he said, waving the poker around expansively before turning and thrusting it into the heart of the fire, sending a fountain of sparks up the chimney.

'I'm here; it's had an impact on me,' I said tentatively, hoping this might help. Joe turned to face me with the poker still in his hand. He looked like he was about to say something but he stopped himself. I got the implication well enough though, and it pissed me off.

'OK, so I may be just a schoolboy,' I said, 'but have you thought about how much worse the world might be if you hadn't made your art? If you hadn't made the effort? If you hadn't marched?'

Joe stood in front of the fire, swaying slightly, flames leaping behind him, and I realised I was fucked. He was such a big guy. He was going to beat me to death with the poker. No one knew where I was, no one would ever find out. All over some dumb statue of a man fucking an otter.

Then just as I had managed to convince myself that he was going to kill me, the poker slipped from his hands and fell onto the hearth with an onomatopoeic clang. I nearly shat my pants. A cryptic expression descended over Joe's face and he looked like he was about to say something again, but instead he slumped to his knees, then toppled forward onto the hearth rug, his head in his hands. As he lay on the floor in front of me, like a great fallen tree, he started crying. Stifled sobs of sadness echoed round the room. I hadn't a clue what to do or say.

Eventually the crying subsided, Joe composed himself and rolled over onto his side, with his back to me.

'Are you OK?' I asked cautiously.

Joe just lay there. 'Mary,' he said, 'is that you?'

'No Joe, it's me, Felix,' I replied cautiously. But Joe didn't say anything. I got up and walked round him to see if he was OK. His eyes were closed; it looked like he was asleep.

*   *   *

223

I was woken early the next morning by a knock on the bedroom door.

'Urrr.'

'Felix, it's Joe.'

I looked at my watch. It was 5.30 a.m. and still dark outside. 'Yeah?' I said nervously, thinking that maybe he wanted to get into bed with me or something. I know that sounds paranoid, but the night before had been a bit weird to say the least, plus this was the man who'd made a statue of a man fucking an otter. Who knew what dark urges seethed in his giant head?

'There's something I think you should see,' he said, which totally didn't put my mind at ease.

'Uh huh . . .'

'There's some breakfast in the kitchen. I'll see you downstairs in ten.'

'OK,' I replied, trying not to sound too relieved. I lay in bed for a couple more minutes, debating what to do. Then figuring that there wasn't much I could do either way, I slipped into my clothes, put the otter into the rucksack and headed downstairs. I'd taken it to bed with me the night before, and I had no intention of letting it out of my sight. Joe was sitting in the kitchen drinking a cup of coffee.

'Felix, I know it's early, but how do you fancy a walk?' The alarm bells started going off again, phrases like, 'shallow grave', 'bummed to death at gunpoint' and 'doesn't want to do the deed in the house' floated through my head.

'But it's still dark,' I said.

'It'll be light soon and it's important to be there at dawn.' I said nothing. 'I'll take that as a yes,' said Joe dryly. 'Do you want some breakfast?'

When we'd finished our breakfast Joe disappeared upstairs, returning a couple of minutes later carrying an anorak.

'Here, you might need a windcheater, it can be a little cool in the mornings round here,' he said handing me the coat. I put it on and then hoisted the rucksack containing the otter over my shoulder. Joe raised an eyebrow, but said nothing.

We walked down the drive to the gate, then down the track a little way, where we turned off onto a narrow trail which led down the hill through the sweet-smelling pines. Joe walked quickly, bounding along on the carpet of dead pine needles that lined the path while I scampered behind in an attempt to keep up. The sky started to brighten. Suddenly Joe stopped and bent down. He picked something up then turned and held it out to me – it was a red Skittle.

'Looks like you got pretty close,' he said, laughing softly. Soon we came to the road, which glistened silver with dew, like the trail of a giant slug. We crossed the road and then plunged back into the woods on the other side where we walked in silence for about fifteen minutes, heading downhill all the time.

I smelt it first, then I heard it and finally, as we rounded a corner in the trail, I saw the silvery sea, sparkling in a little rocky cove, like a hundred million diamonds in a very big bucket.

When we reached the shore Joe stopped again, turned to me, held his index finger to his lips and pointed over to the rocks on the far side of the bay. Then we skirted

225

along the edge of the small ribbon of beach, the soft sand murmuring beneath our feet. After clambering onto the rocks Joe crouched down, indicating to me silently that I should do the same. Then we did this awkward crab-like shuffle to the end of the point, and I was starting to get a little pissed off with the whole thing when he stopped and turned to me, his eyes twinkling.

In front of us a group of otters lay on their backs in the glassy water, surrounded by long strands of thick, flat seaweed. We sat and watched as they fished. When they found a likely snack they would return to the surface and break the shells open on rocks they held on their stomachs as they lay on their backs in the water. It was amazing. I had no idea they did that. While the older otters fished, the youngsters played amongst them occasionally eliciting the odd admonitory snap from their elders when their antics became too reckless.

I don't know how long we sat and watched the otters, but there was real heat in the sun when Joe indicated that we should leave. I stood up; Joe made a grab for my arm, but missed. The otters spotted me, arched their smooth, dark backs and disappeared below the surface. Joe glared at me, but I knew what I was doing. I reached into my rucksack and pulled out the statue. Joe stood up. I looked out to sea. The otters had resurfaced some way off, near a group of rocks further out from the shore. I held the statue up with one hand and then tucked it under my chin and leaned back. I looked over at Joe; he smiled and nodded. Then I shot-putted it with all my might. It described a neat arc through the clear morning air before falling into the turquoise water with a resonant plunk. I glimpsed a final flash of glittery pink as the sun caught it one last time before it sunk into the tangled depths of the kelp forest.

When we got back to the house Joe made a fresh pot of coffee. We took it out onto the deck.

'Mary loved the otters, you know,' said Joe.

'Is she the lady in the paintings?' I asked without really thinking.

A look of surprise crossed Joe's face. 'How do you know . . . ?'

'When I went for a shower I got the wrong room. I'm sorry.'

Joe looked at me. 'Yes she is Felix. Mary was my wife. She died in 1996.'

I didn't know what to say, but that was OK because Joe kept on going. He told me about Mary, how she was his second wife, how they'd been married five years when she was diagnosed with breast cancer, how the cancer was quick and merciless and how Mary was dead within six months. When he finished we sat in silence for a little while and drank our coffee.

'Are the pictures in the room, are they what you've been doing since you gave up art?' I said, realising as I did that it had come out all wrong. 'You know, they're very good,' I said hastily, in a lame attempt to rectify my mistake. Fortunately Joe saw the funny side. He shook his head and laughed.

The bus to San Francisco left from the town square at four in the afternoon. Joe offered to drive me all the way to the airport, but I didn't want to put him to the trouble. Besides, I wanted to be alone. I had a lot to think about.

227

'Look, I hope things go well with . . . er . . . the "A" Levels, and I'm sorry if I was a little crazy at times. No hard feelings, right?' said Joe as we waited in the square for the bus.

I shrugged. Fucking 'A' Levels, I'd totally forgotten about them. Two weeks ago the whole 'A' Level thing felt like this huge asteroid that was about to smash into the earth, now it was gone, just a speck of dust on the telescope lens of some sheepish astronomer. In fact, as I sat there in Joe's old Volvo, my life back home seemed impossibly remote.

The bus picked up speed as it crested the hill at the top of the valley; I looked back down on the neat little town of Puerto Novo and then settled back for the ride. The bus rolled along the coast and then turned inland. I sat and watched the fruit farms of the San Joaquin valley rush past me, as they hurried to get home before nightfall.

We pressed on into the dusk. The sky smudged red, then purple, then a deep blue-black. The bright strip lights inside the bus flickered into life. I looked out the window, but the view was obscured by the reflection of the inside of the bus; a ghostly, parallel world rushing along beside us in the late evening. In the reflection I could see that a couple sitting in front of me had their hands down each other's trousers, unaware that they could be seen from that angle. As I watched them I started to get a hard-on, but feeling ashamed, I looked away. The roads gradually grew bigger, the traffic growing to a swollen torrent, rushing to break over San Francisco.

*

The morning after I fed Vespasian the laxatives, I turned up at Mrs Pretzel's at the usual time. I rang the bell and waited. After five minutes there was still no sign of Mrs P so I decided to have a look around the back. The patio doors were open, I knocked, shouted a hello and then poked my head into the kitchen. Over by the big stove I spotted Mrs P kneeling on the floor, next to Vespasian who was lying on his side on some newspaper. The room stank. My stomach lurched unpleasantly.

'Mrs Pretzel, it's Felix, is everything OK?' I asked.

Still kneeling, she turned and looked at me vaguely. Blurry rainbows of make-up ran down the weathered features of her face.

'What's wrong?' I asked stepping into the kitchen.

'It's Vespasian, Felix, he's dying . . .' she sobbed.

The smell was awful. I felt sick. I held my hand over my mouth and stepped back into the garden, where, after a bit of ringing around, I managed to get hold of a vet.

The vet was a middle-aged woman with long, straight, black hair and big, thick glasses. I showed her into the kitchen where she examined Vespasian. After some head-shaking and tutting she left, taking Vespasian with her. Mrs P wanted to go too, but the vet said there was no point.

After I'd helped the vet carry Vespasian to the car, I returned to the kitchen. Mrs P was nowhere to be seen. I found her out on the patio, sitting at the table, pounding a glass of sherry. She had stopped crying. As I sat down she poured herself another glass and knocked it back. She was obviously intent on getting totally hammered. I wasn't sure what to do. To begin with I just sat there and tried my best to be supportive, but the more she drank, the more random she got.

229

'I could have been a vet if I'd had the opportunity,' she said, 'then I'd have been able to save Vespasian myself.' I nodded sympathetically. 'Youngsters today don't know what they've got. Everything's handed to you on a plate. You think life is just one big primrose path. In my day, there weren't the opportunities and of course there was the war, not that anyone remembers that nowadays . . .'

She polished off the bottle of sherry in less than half an hour. Then she told me to go and get her another from her stash in the pantry. I wasn't sure what to do, but I didn't think that I should be giving her more sherry.

'Are you sure you haven't had enough?' I asked hesitantly.

'Enough?' she said fixing me with an icy stare, 'I'll be the judge of when I've had enough. Now are you going to get me the sherry or do I have to get it myself?'

I called Dora from the pantry and told her what had happened.

'OK Felix, I've got to drop Jemima and Rollo at nursery. I'll be around as soon as I can.'

Back on the patio I placed the bottle on the table and sat down. Mrs P leaned over unsteadily and poured herself a big glass.

'What'll I do without Vespasian? I've had him since Aubrey left . . . and now he's with that slut in Maidenhead,' she wailed.

I was confused. I didn't think the vet looked like a slut. She looked like a perfectly respectable middle-aged woman. Plus, I was sure she was local. Maidenhead was like twenty miles away.

'Sorry, you mean Vesp—'

'No Felix you silly boy, I mean Aubrey, my ex-husband Aubrey.'

'But Aubrey's dead remember,' I said, figuring that the shock must have been too great for her and her mind had finally caved in.

'No he's not, Aubrey's not dead. He's very much alive.'

'But who's in the urn?'

'He left me fifteen years ago,' replied Mrs P, ignoring my (rather stupid) question, 'he left me and married that strumpet secretary of his. She's twenty years younger than him. Twenty years younger than me.'

My mind was reeling.

'I know what you're thinking,' she said, accusatorily, 'she's a mad old bat, pretending her husband's dead, but you don't know what it's like to have your husband of thirty years walk out on you for some . . . some type-writing whore. Oh, I know everything's different these days, it's all free love and everyone lets it all hang out, but I'm from a different generation.'

So Aubrey was alive. That explained her reluctance to talk about him.

As she rambled on and drank more, I started to get quite worried. Fortunately, just as I was starting to panic, Dora appeared and took control. She put Mrs P to bed and then I helped her clean up the kitchen. I'll spare you the details, but it wasn't a pleasant job.

'Thanks Felix,' said Dora when we'd finished.

'What for?' I asked, peeling off my rubber gloves and dropping them in the bin bag which sat in the middle of the kitchen floor.

'Thanks for being so good with my mother-in-law, I know she can be quite difficult sometimes.'

231

I was like, 'Mrs P, difficult? No. You've got the wrong person.'

'That's OK,' I said.

'I know she's very fond of you.'

Which was simultaneously flattering, implausible and ever so slightly creepy. I mean, if she was so fond of me then why was she cheating me out of my pay?

'Yes, she looks forward to you coming round. I've seen a great improvement in her attitude since you've been working for her.'

If Dora knew that I was responsible for Vespasian's condition and had wanted to make me feel as guilty as possible she couldn't have done a better job.

I shrugged.

Dora leaned over and tied the corners of the bin bag together, and she was just about to lift it out onto the patio when she spotted something on the floor beside it. She bent down, picked it up and held it out to me. On her dimpled, yellow, rubber palm sat the missing Z.

*

In San Francisco I caught a cab down to the airport hotel and checked in, paying with money Joe had given me to help me get home.

It was still fairly early when I got up to my room, so I switched on the TV, but all that seemed to be on was wall-to-wall adverts. In the end I found an episode of *The Simpsons*, but after watching it for an hour it still hadn't finished because of all the ads, so I switched it off. It was utterly gruelling. I reckon US TV is the worst in the world. Seriously, it's worse than Chinese TV, fuck, it's even worse than French TV.

Whatever.

The flight left early the next morning, so I set the alarm on my mobile and fell straight into a deep, dreamless sleep.

The next morning I found my seat on the plane to Newark, and I was just getting the diary out to update it when I heard a voice.

'Hey . . . is this seat forty-one?'

'Uh, yeah,' I said, smiling at the young girl who stood in front of me scratching her head. She was cute, in a demi-goth kind of way. I mean, she was dressed in black from head to toe, but without the full-on goth hair and make-up. She did have a nose stud and she was wearing a NIN T-shirt, but you could see she was kind of dabbling.

'Then it looks like we're going to be travelling together for the next five hours,' she said, standing on her tiptoes and putting her bag in the overhead locker. Her T-shirt scurried up her torso exposing a hard, flat stomach with a pierced belly button. The natives started getting restless, so I placed the diary strategically on my lap. She closed the locker and flopped down next to me.

'I tell ya, flying's such a fucking drag these days after that whole 9/11 shit,' she said wearily. I nodded. She sat up. 'What's your name?' she asked.

'Felix.'

'Where ya from Felix?'

'England.'

'No shit. What ya doing in the US?'

'Oh . . . it's a long story,' I replied as a stewardess appeared to do the whole seat belt, chair in the upright position check thing.

'What's your name?' I asked when the stewardess had moved on.

'Raleigh. Pleased to meet ya Felix,' she said, fiddling with an MP3 player which she'd pulled from her jacket pocket.

We'd been in the air for about an hour when Raleigh hoiked out her earphones and turned to me.

'So Felix, ya never did tell me how come you're over here.' In the absence of anything better to do, I told her. As I did a look of scepticism spread over her face.

'You're not shitting me?' she said after I'd finished.

'You think I could make this kind of thing up?' I replied staring back at her.

'Felix that's some fucking story. Man, tell me about that bit with the guy with the gun in China again.' So I did. 'What ya doing in New York?' she asked when I'd finished.

'Oh, I'm not going, it's just a short stopover in Newark. I fly on to the UK this evening.'

'Pity,' she said thoughtfully.

'What are you doing in New York?' I asked.

'I'm there with my band,' she said.

'What kind of music do you play?' I asked.

'Well, it's like a goth thing, but on a kind of old-skool hip-hop tip,' she said without a trace of irony. 'Yeah, we're off to New York to like meet with this sportswear company who want to sign us up for a tour of like snow-boarding resorts this winter. They want the brand to be a bit more edgy.'

'That sounds cool,' I replied inanely.

'Yeah, like I've never snowboarded before, but, if we sign they'll give us a bunch of free gear, pay for lessons and shit . . . look, Felix, have you ever done it on a plane before?'

'What, you mean snowboarding?'

She cracked up. 'No, stoopid . . . you know . . . *it* . . .'

I felt totally embarrassed. I shrugged, I mean, what was I going to say? 'I haven't even done *it* on the fucking ground.' I think not.

'You wanna?' she said, smiling conspiratorially. I shrugged again. Which she totally took as a yes.

'OK . . . I'll go to the john, you follow me in like two minutes, knock three times and I'll let you in,' she said, standing up and winking.

A hundred and twenty elephants later I stood up, then lurched down the aisle desperately trying to conceal the boner which was by now raging out of control in my kecks. When I got to the bog, I knocked on the door, it opened quickly, Raleigh pulled me in and locked the door. She had stripped down to her bra and knickers, which were of course black. She grabbed me and stuck her hot, flexuous tongue down my throat and started fiddling with my fly. Man, I was so excited I thought my knob was going to burst.

'What about protection?' I asked, pulling away from her a little.

'Don't worry I've got some,' she said huskily, nodding at a condom which lay on the side of the basin. 'Come on Felix we've got to hurry, we can't take too much time, in case we get caught.'

Which was like no problem for me, being a sixteen-year-old virgin on a permanent sexual hair trigger and everything. Technically speaking I popped my cherry

30,000 feet over Colorado or wherever, but, I tell you now, it was a pretty close-run thing; it can't have lasted more than a few seconds. Not that Raleigh seemed to mind; when it was over she just pulled her clothes on, adjusted her hair and walked out the door. And that was that. I sat on the toilet for a couple of minutes filled with a strange sense of defeat. I mean, I felt as if I should be acting like a footballer who's just scored a goal, but I just didn't feel that way. Somehow, it didn't seem as significant as I thought it might.

I got back to my seat a few minutes later to find Raleigh plugged back into her MP3 player. She smiled at me as I sat down and then went back to reading her magazine.

I looked out of the window as America unfurled below me. I watched as the rugged wilderness of mountains, forests and rivers made way for the huge, empty plains of the Midwest. We passed over a big city, which looked like a culture on a Petri dish; a large, grey bacterial blob consuming the green land around it. Then I must have fallen asleep because I dreamt that Miko was cutting my hair and that my hair was falling from the plane to the ground below, falling on the citizens of Bacteria City, falling on the golden oceans of corn, falling on the eskers and oxbow lakes, the car salesrooms and hospitals.

I was woken by the pilot announcing the start of our descent into Newark. Raleigh chatted away through the landing, talking about a party she was going to that night in some club I'd never heard of and if I thought she should get her traguses pierced. I said she should, despite the fact that I have no idea what a tragus is. Not that it mattered, she wasn't really listening to me anyway.

Airports suck. They're all the fucking same. The four hours I had to wait for my connecting flight to the UK seemed to drag on for ever. I spent the time roaming restlessly around the air conditioned, marble-floored, glass and steel box, from coffee bar to newsagent to coffee bar. I'd had enough of travelling. I just wanted to get home. I wanted to eat familiar foods. I wanted to be able to wear some different clothes. I wanted to sit for an evening playing video games, shooting the breeze with Jim.

After what seemed like an eternity they called my flight.

Fuck. You would not believe what happened about two hours ago, just after I boarded the plane in Newark. I was getting comfortable and everything, when who should walk down the aisle, but my fucking mother and her fucking mate Sandra! I'd completely forgotten that she was in the States. Fortunately, I saw them before they saw me, so I slouched down in my seat and pulled the hood of my hoody up over my face, like I was trying to sleep or something, leaving just enough of a gap to keep an eye on them. Luckily, they had seats some way in front of me.

I watched as they stowed their hand luggage in the overhead locker. And then, just before they sat down, it happened. They kissed. And when I say they kissed, I'm talking about a full-on sexual, passionate, spit-swapping, tonsillectomy type affair, not a platonic peck on the cheek.

My fear of discovery morphed into a big, silvery pool

of righteous indignation. I was like, 'Fucking hell, my mum's a lezzer.' When did that happen? She totally didn't seem the sort . . . whatever that is . . . OK, so I've never met a lesbian before, or at least not knowingly. I've seen them in action of course, but to be honest I'm not too sure that Rob's extensive collection of literature and films on the subject is a particularly accurate reflection of reality.

I was still reeling from the whole Sapphic mother revelation when this middle-aged couple appeared in the aisle beside me. The woman was dressed in an expensive grey wool suit, her hair hovered over her head like a fibreglass helmet, held aloft by about ten gallons of hairspray, her scrawny, sun-dried hands and neck dripping with gold jewellery.

The man was short, fat and bald with a squashed nose and a cauliflower ear. He wore a dark blue blazer, chinos and a pair of deck shoes. The woman scanned her ticket, and scowled at me, with a look that clearly indicated that she thought I might have a bomb in my shoe or something. She pouted and looked at her ticket again. There was a terse little whispered exchange with her partner in which she totally made him change seats.

'Hello,' he said, after he'd sat down next to me, 'Bernard Mandley. Pleased to meet you.' His voice was warm, a friendly smile played on his lips.

'Oh, yeah hi, I'm fine thank you,' I answered a little absently, keeping the whole slouched down thing going on, on account of the proximity of my mother and her lesbian lover, 'how are you?'

'Very well thank you,' replied Bernard, 'we have just enjoyed a short holiday in New York.'

238

'Yes,' said the horror show, taking her seat, 'New York really is such a marvellous city.'

'I didn't go,' I said abruptly.

'Right . . . so where have you been?' she asked haughtily.

'Hong Kong, China, Tokyo, LA, San Francisco and now here,' I replied through gritted teeth, not wanting to deal with her shit, but somehow getting sucked in anyway.

'Oh,' she said, clearly a little taken aback. Then she smiled a big motherfucker of a fake smile. 'Are you on one of those cheap round-the-world tickets,' she said, with the emphasis distinctly on the cheap. I thought about it and then nodded, refusing to bite at the little fly she'd cast. She smiled and sat back in her seat.

'Yes,' said Bernard hastily, evidently sensing the tension between myself and his good wife, 'it's nice to get some time off. Cost me a fortune of course, but then there are no pockets in shrouds, are there?' he said, guffawing loudly. I shrugged. 'Margaret spent a small fortune in Bloomingdale's.'

'Oh, now come on Bernard, it wasn't that much,' said his wife in an annoyed tone. I didn't reply so we all lapsed into a slightly uncomfortable silence, which suited me just fine. I was happy to maintain a low profile.

The plane had just moved off the stand when it occurred to me that I had somehow to get home before my mother when we landed, so I could be back in time for the 'A' Level results party. I pulled out my mobile phone, Margaret spotted this and shot another filthy look in my direction. I ignored her and sent a text message to Jim to the effect that he had to meet me at

239

Heathrow, avoid running into my mother and be on time, etc.

*

Two weeks after the Maxi incident, my father turned up at the house to take us out again. I was playing *Half Life* on the computer in my bedroom.

'Felix, your father's here,' shouted my mother up the stairs.

Deep in the bowels of the Black Mesa Research Labs, I lobbed a fragmentation grenade onto a seemingly empty landing.

'Felix, your father's here,' shouted my mother again.

I counted to five. The grenade exploded. Chunks of headcrab flesh spattered the walls. I turned the corner and sprayed a few rounds down the corridor just in case.

'Felix come down now,' she shouted angrily. I ignored her again. After a brief pause I heard footsteps on the stair. I stowed my machine gun and pulled out my RPG launcher.

'Felix, can I come in?' It was my father at the door. I ignored him and ran down to the next corner. 'Felix, I'm sorry about last time, it was an accident. I'll make sure it never happens again,' he said, his voice muffled by the door. I sidestepped out into the corridor and fired off two RPGs. Unfortunately, one of the assassins was standing just round the corner, right in front of me. The backblast from my own RPG killed me instantly.

'Felix . . .' My father's voice sounded pained. I got up and opened the door.

'I'm not going to any lameoid ice spectacular,' I said.

'But what about Louise, she's looking forward—'

'No she's not, she's just happy to be with you, she

doesn't care about a bunch of idiots on skates dressed up in animal costumes.'

'I'm sorry,' he said, 'but it's important that you and Jill are friends, we're going to be together.'

'What, like you and mum were?'

He looked at the ground. 'Felix, what can I do . . . what . . .'

'Well for a start I don't want to go to another safari park, model village or ice spectacular. Can't we just go round to yours and be normal?'

'But I thought you and Louise liked—'

'Dad . . .'

So we went round to Jill's house. Where we watched TV, played a game of Monopoly (which I won), and generally behaved like a normal family. Jill made us chicken nuggets for tea (which is something my mother never made us at home) and then we watched *Shrek* on DVD.

I'm not saying it was perfect; I could tell that Jill was a little pissed off about my insistence that Maximillian, Liege of the Faerie Kings, be banished to the garden, but it was a start.

*

We'd been in the air for about two hours and the waitresses were clearing away the remains of our meal when Bernard asked me what I did. I told him about my 'A' Levels and my offer to study law at Cambridge.

'Our oldest, Ben, he's a lawyer in the City. Hopes to make partner next year,' he said. I nodded, not really wishing to pursue the conversation. The plane was pretty quiet, what with people starting to go to sleep, and there was the distinct possibility that my mother would hear me.

241

'I don't know much about the law,' he continued, 'but I'd say it's a pretty good racket, judging by the amount my shyster charges me for writing a letter,' he said, laughing loudly. A couple of people turned round in their seats to see where the noise was coming from, I slouched back down in my seat and pulled up my hoody.

'I'm in management consultancy myself,' said Bernard, oblivious to the fact that I wasn't up for a chat, 'CEO of a small company based in Guildford. We do a lot of training work, that sort of thing. It's been pretty successful in the last few years. Mind you, it's just as well, because Margaret spends it as quickly as I can make it,' he said, leaning over and winking at me.

'Bernard, really, you know that's not true,' protested Margaret.

'Nothing wrong with that dear, good for the country I say. I can think of several shops in Guildford that would go out of business tomorrow if it weren't for our Margaret.'

'Bernard, you're talking absolute nonsense. How much of that wine did you have with the meal?'

'No . . . Margaret . . . I'm making a serious point,' said Bernard, suddenly looking serious, to emphasise the seriousity of the serious point he was making, 'what's good for us is good for everyone else. It's the notion that underpins our whole economic system.'

'Oh Bernard, I do wish you'd shut up,' she said, pulling on this diamante-studded black velvet eye mask that she produced from her handbag. Presumably the one provided by the airline wasn't good enough for her.

'I'm going to sleep, and I suggest you do too,' she said, reaching to her side and pushing the chair back into its fully reclined position.

BACK HOME

When we landed, I had to wait for my mum and Sandra to get off first, which meant I was about the last off the plane. I dawdled through immigration and, as I only had hand luggage, I zipped past them as they were waiting at the carousel in baggage reclaim.

In arrivals, Jim was standing next to a bin, struggling to juggle looking cool while staying out of sight of my mother.

'Jim . . . we need to hurry.' He drove like a mother-fucker up the motorway while I told him the story of my trip.

'Let me get this straight Felix,' he said after I'd finished, 'you're telling me that the otter was made by Joe Banks, that it was worth over a million dollars and that you threw it in the sea?'

'Yep.'

'Bullshit,' said Jim emphatically, 'complete and utter bullshit.'

'You've heard of him though?' I asked.

'Of course, he's only like the fucking daddy of American art.' Then he asked me a billion questions, about Joe and the statue and my trip. I don't blame him,

I have been known to exaggerate shit. Plus, as I was telling him about Mr Huai and Joe and Miko, part of me started wondering if the whole thing had really happened.

'What proof have you got?' asked Jim as we turned off the motorway. I dug out my passport and showed him the stamps from Hong Kong, China, Japan and the US. He was still pretty sceptical.

'OK, so you did go round the world, but that doesn't mean you met Joe Banks.' I was like, 'Whatever.' I had other more important things on my mind at that moment.

When we arrived back at the close, Jim edged the car slowly up to my house just in case my mother had somehow miraculously got back before us, but she hadn't: the drive was empty. Aware that I didn't have much time before she got home, I jumped out of the car, put the key in the front door and turned, but it wouldn't work. I couldn't understand it. I tried the handle and the door swung open; in front of me stood my sister holding two pieces of paper, one in either hand.

'Welcome home Felix,' she said, this big smug grin smeared over her face like the cheap make-up of which she is so fond. Something in the tone of her voice told me that I was in deep shit.

'I can't believe you opened my fucking mail,' I said indignantly. My sister sat slouched across an armchair drinking a can of Diet Coke, though I don't know how because she was still grinning from one motherfucking ear to the other.

'Felix, Felix, Felix,' she said in a patronising tone, 'I can't believe you've just been round the world, blowing like £3,550 of your university fund,' she continued, totally mimicking my voice, but in a kind of whiny way which really pissed me off.

'Grow up.'

'Don't worry, Felix, I will, and when I do you may just be allowed out of the house again after Mum finds out about your little trip.'

As she finished talking, I leapt from my chair like a jungle cat, snatched the bank statement from her hand and ripped it in two. She just sat there smirking. Perplexed, I looked at the statement; it was a photocopy. Evidently she wasn't fucking around.

'Felix, enough of this game; tell me the truth,' she said in a totally harsh voice, the smile suddenly disappearing from her face. Sometimes she so totally takes after my mother it's scary.

What could I do? Apart from lie like a motherfucker. So, I told her this heavily sanitised version of events, which I'd sort of semi-rehearsed in case I had to phone my mother in San Francisco. I explained that Jim had dared me to go round the world after I lost a bet on a game of *Mario Carts*. It was a terrible lie, but I didn't have much room for manoeuvre, plus I was aware that my mother could pitch up at any moment.

When I finished I could see my sister was impressed. After all, I suppose it was quite a gesture, just getting on a plane and fucking off around the world for two weeks.

'I so can't believe that you just did that Felix,' she said, eyeing me suspiciously, 'it's totally not like you.' I shrugged. 'I still think you're like hiding something. I must have heard your speech on the evils of gap years about a million times, plus you almost had a nervous break-down after a couple of weeks in France.'

247

I was like 'What. The. Fuck?' That stuff about France was such bullshit.

'Yeah and how come the bill's paid off, where did you get the money?' she asked like she was Miss fucking Marple or something.

I hadn't even looked. So the money had gone through. At least that was one thing. I looked at the bill, and smiled: not only was the bill paid off, but I was £2,000 better off. Joe had been as good as his word.

'I've been saving . . . you know, the money I made working in Mrs Pretzel's garden.'

She sat up. 'No way. From what Mum said, Mrs Pretzel was ripping you off left, right and centre. You couldn't have made a tenth of that money working for her.'

I was outraged. How did my sister know that? And what's more, if my mother knew that I was getting ripped off, why hadn't she done anything about it?

'And I have also saved quite a lot in the last couple of years.'

'Yeah, like right,' she said sceptically, 'from what exactly?'

'I've been dealing in *Star Wars* figures on eBay. It all adds up.'

She snorted. 'Felix, you are always skint. You did not make, what . . . £5,000 dealing in *Star Wars* figures on the internet. And anyway, who's this Joseph Banks character who transferred all this money?' Jim's jaw dropped quicker than Kelly Livermore's knickers after half a bottle of Aftershock. I smiled at him knowingly.

My sister was quite right, I never even made five pence dealing in *Star Wars* figures. It was true that I had tried to sell Princess Leia and a couple of stormtroopers after reading in this magazine that *Star Wars* figures could be worth like mega money. But I never sold them, possibly on account of the fact that the stormtroopers' helmets were painted with pink nail polish and Princess Leia had been chewed a little by Maximillian, Liege of the Faerie Kings.

'And you like just decided to spend all this hard-earned cash because you were bored and Jim dared you. I so believe that one . . . like not.' As she said this my mother's car pulled into the drive. I was like 'Oh, shit.'

'Look, if you keep quiet I think we can do a deal,' I said hurriedly.

'What do you mean?'

'You still want a horse?'

'UH HUH.'

'How much does one cost?'

My sister looked thoughtful.

'Hurry up . . .' I said, my heart starting to mosh up and down in my chest.

'I don't know . . . I guess a couple of thousand would be about right,' she said, a smile spreading over her face. I didn't even attempt to argue, she had me right where she wanted me.

'It's a deal.' She looked totally sceptical. 'Please,' I pleaded, 'if you don't like the terms you can tell Mum later, just don't say anything now.'

My mother swept into the room like a hurricane making landfall, depositing carrier bags, suitcases and clothing on every available surface. Then there were all sorts of kisses and hugs and shit.

'Well?' she said after things had calmed down a little. We all stood there blankly. 'What have you three been up to?' she asked suspiciously, her spider senses picking up the slight unease in the room.

'Nothing,' I said hastily, but I must have been a fraction too quick off the mark because she was onto me like a motherfucker.

'Felix . . . what's been going on?' she said sharply.

'Eh, nothing, I swear . . . unless you include me travelling round the world, hanging out with famous artists, gangsters, rock musicians . . . you know, the usual.'

'Oh, Felix, you've got such a sense of humour,' she said, pinching my cheek just a little too hard, like she was Don Corleone or something. 'So how's the cold?'

'Oh, much better thank you Mummm . . . oowww.'

'Oh well that's good to hear,' she said, letting go, her voice smothered in that squirty kind of sarcasm you get from a can.

'Louise, what's Felix been up to?' she said turning to my sister. My heart leapt into my mouth, poised to stage-dive onto the carpet in front of me.

'I'm not sure; I think he's been ill, he looked pretty bad when I got here last night, though he seems a lot better today.' My heartbeat slowed. I could see that my mother was not entirely convinced, but she certainly didn't want to entertain the thought that her darling daughter might be involved in one of my nefarious schemes. She looked around the room. Then she looked back at me.

'So, then . . . what's the news?'

I shrugged. 'Sorry . . . what do you mean?'

'Your "A" Levels silly.'

I realised that I hadn't even looked at the results. I picked up the opened envelope from the table, where

Louise had left it, and handed it to her nervously, hoping she wouldn't ask me what I got before I had a chance to look at them.

*

The Paris Peace Conference opened on January 12, 1919 and a series of meetings were held in and around the city for just over a year. These meetings were attended by the leaders of thirty-two states. However, practically speaking, the proceedings were dominated by the five major powers who had fought the Germans in World War I: Britain, France, the United States, Italy and Japan.

Present in my bedroom that afternoon were me and my sister, with Jim acting in an unofficial peace-keeper/observer type role.

Five treaties resulted from the meetings in France dealing with the obligations of the defeated powers. The main terms of these treaties, which are referred to collectively as the Treaty of Versailles, are as follows:

(1) the surrender of the entire German empire;
(2) the return of Alsace-Lorraine;
(3) the succession of Eupen-Malmedy to Belgium, Memel to Lithuania, and Hultschin to Czechoslovakia;
(4) the same for Poznania, parts of East Prussia and Upper Silesia to Poland;
(5) the restoration of freedom in Danzig;
(6) plebiscites to be held in northern Schleswig to resolve frontier issues;
(7) occupation and special status for the Saar;
(8) demilitarisation and occupation of the Rhineland;

251

(9) German financial reparations of £6,600 million;

(10) a ban on the union of Germany and Austria;

(11) German acceptance of guilt in causing the war;

(12) provision for the trial of the former Kaiser and others;

(13) serious limitation of the German army;

(14) serious limitation of the German navy.

Trust me, I wrote an essay on that shit in my exams. Whatever.

The main terms of the historic treaty of Felix's bedroom, August 2003, were as follows:

(1) Louise to destroy the bank statement and all copies thereof;

(2) Felix to pay Louise reparations of £2,020;

(3) Neither party to discuss the agreement with anyone outside those present in the bedroom.

What could I do? She drives a hard bargain. If I didn't agree she'd grass me up and she had material evidence.

The £2,020 was the balance of the $10,000 Joe transferred into the emergency account, which coincidentally enough, happened to be the exact sum of money she needed to buy a horse and pay for its upkeep. Quite how she expects to get around my mother and explain how she got the money I do not know, but as we have just seen she's a devious little motherfucker and I'm sure she'll find a way. In return she destroyed the statement and all copies in front of me, and I don't think she'll grass, because it would throw a spotlight onto the origin of the

252

£2,020 and she'd have to answer all sorts of uncomfortable questions which might well jeopardise the whole pony scenario.

Contrary to my expectations the party was pretty good fun. Loads of people turned up: Jim, Kevin, my mother, my aunts, Julie and Tim, Dora and the whole sick Women of Achievement crew. The only no-shows were Mrs P and Rob. Jim told me that Rob had been grounded indefinitely by his father for failing all of his 'A' Levels.

About an hour into the party a car pulled into the close. It was my dad and Jill.

'So Felix, come on, what did you get,' asked my dad as he got out of the car, an excited look on his face.

'Er, four As.'

He punched the air, and then hugged me. It was a bit embarrassing, what with Jim and Kevin and everyone watching, but still.

'So, off to Cambridge then,' he said letting go of me. I nodded.

A little while later, Jim informed me he was in desperate need of a blaze, so we snuck upstairs. Jim hung out the window with the spliff as I checked my e-mail. There was one from Miko. I was reading it when my mother shouted up the stairs.

'Felix, Jim. I'd like to speak to you both.'

An electromagnetic wave of guilt pulsed through my body.

'He can't be dead,' I said for the second time.

'I'm sorry Felix, but you must understand that he was old and he was very ill,' said my mother sympathetically, mistaking my guilt for grief.

'But I thought he was over that, I thought he was getting better.'

'Apparently he had a relapse.'

I was about to go, 'I know, he had a . . .' when I realised what my mother had just said.

'What about Mrs Pretzel, how's she?' asked Jim.

'She's upset. The dog was very important to her,' replied my mother.

'And what about the gardening,' I asked, 'does she still want me to go tomorrow?'

My mother nodded. 'Yes, in fact she'd like you both to go over tomorrow,' she replied, looking at Jim.

When the party was over and everyone had left, I helped my mother tidy up. I still felt guilty as a motherfucker.

'How was the US?' I asked as we carried the garden table into the garage.

'Yes, it was great . . . great to get away,' said my mother thoughtfully.

'I won't take that as an insult . . .' I said, smiling. My mother smiled back and shook her head. 'How's Sa—'

My mother looked at me. 'What? How's what, Felix?'

'Nothing, don't worry,' I said, closing the garage door. I was going to ask about Sandra, but then I stopped myself. I figure that what my mother does with her life is her business and I suppose she'll tell us when she's ready.

After we tidied up outside, we moved into the kitchen and started clearing away the dirty dishes.

'You know, I've been thinking,' I said to my mother, who was loading the dishwasher.

She stood up. 'Yes?'

'I'm not sure I'm going to study law.'

'What do you mean?'

'Well, I've never been that interested in law.'

'But what are you going to do instead?' she asked.

'I'm not sure . . . I think I'll look to change courses.'

'Doing what?'

'I don't know yet.'

She looked at me and smiled again. 'You could take a gap year.'

'Umm, I'm not sure . . .'

'In fact, I think I've still got the gap-year brochures.'

'Thanks Mum, but can we talk about it in the morning? I'm feeling a bit knackered. I didn't sleep much on the plane last night.'

'Sorry, what plane?' she asked sharply.

Fortunately, I kept my cool. 'You . . . I'm sure *you* didn't sleep much on the plane last night.'

My mum looked at me suspiciously and then smiled. 'You're right, it's been a big day for all of us . . . let's talk about it tomorrow.'

Upstairs in my bedroom, as I unpacked my rucksack, I was surprised to find just how much random junk I'd managed to accumulate. I found the flyer from the Hong Kong tailor, some Yen, the map of San Francisco, plane tickets . . . all sorts of stuff. As I sat on my bed and looked at these things I thought about Miss Frances and Mr Huai, Miko and Joe and everything that had happened in the last two weeks. A little later, however, as I lay in my bed, on the soft sand of sleep's shore, it was the statue that I thought of. The bald man and the glittery otter lying on the sea bed, locked together, possibly already home to limpets and sea anemones, subject to the occasional curious inspection by one of the family of otters as it searched for food amongst the thick, rubbery trunks of the kelp forest.

As I drifted off to sleep, it occurred to me that I never did find out what it meant.

The next day we buried Vespasian in a grave that Jim and I dug at the bottom of the garden. Mrs Pretzel recited 'The Lake Isle of Innisfree' by WB Yeats and then cried a bit. Afterwards we held a little wake, with some crisps and a couple of bottles of Mrs P's sherry.

Jim and I both worked for Mrs P for what was left of the summer, and by the time we'd finished the garden was looking pretty immaculate.

Mrs Pretzel didn't change a great deal, in fact in some ways she was worse, because Jim was her big favourite and she used to try and play him off against me. However, somehow her antics didn't bug me like they had before. I even let her win at Scrabble. I still felt guilty about Vespasian.

Mrs P never mentioned Aubrey's resurrection again, but I did notice that the urn had disappeared from the drawing room mantelpiece. I tried to find out more about Aubrey from my mother, but she said she didn't know anything and she refused to ask Dora.

In other news, my sister has kept her trap shut and has just about finished lining mum up on the pony front, though I am starting to tire of her constantly referring to me as her 'bitch'.

Whatever.

Just before Jim and me finished working in the garden, Dora bought Mrs Pretzel a puppy: another Cavalier King Charles Spaniel, which Mrs P decided to call Titus.

Titus is every bit as stupid as Vespasian was. Mrs P loves him very much.

Acknowledgements

With thanks to my mother and father, Richard and Susan; my sisters, Rosie, Joey and Gillian; David and all at DGA; Jason, Rachel, Roger, Suzanne, Sue, Claire, Angus and all at Vintage; Ben, Molly, Stew, Anne, Al, Rita, The Tar, Denise, Simon, Jono, Pauline, Richie, Juan, Van, Tom, Nik Nak, Simon, Iwona, Peter, Liz, Big Jim and Ches.

www.randomhouse.co.uk/vintage